About the Author

James Bovill is an examiner for the IBO. Until he retired some years ago, he worked as a secondary teacher in the Glasgow area, where he still lives. He has three daughters, three grandchildren, and since 2009, has enjoyed the companionship of a lady from New Jersey, USA. He claims to be influenced by Bob Dylan, Mervyn Peake and Evelyn Waugh, who help him to laugh; and Damon Runyon, who helps him to cry. He describes his fifth novel, *The Tale of Franklin Gaddarini,* as a meditation.

By the Same Author

Making a Stand,
Cousins,
Private Investigations,
Saul of Solway.

THE TALE OF FRANKLIN GADDARINI

"The man lived in the tombs and no-one could secure him anymore, even with a chain."

James Bovill

THE TALE OF
FRANKLIN GADDARINI

Vanguard Press

VANGUARD PAPERBACK

© Copyright **2024**
James Bovill

The right of James Bovill to be identified as author of
this work has been asserted by him in accordance with the
Copyright, Designs and Patents Act 1988.

All Rights Reserved

No reproduction, copy or transmission of this publication
may be made without written permission.
No paragraph of this publication may be reproduced,
copied or transmitted save with the written permission of the
publisher, or in accordance with the provisions
of the Copyright Act 1956 (as amended).

Any person who commits any unauthorised act in relation to
this publication may be liable to criminal
prosecution and civil claims for damages.

A CIP catalogue record for this title is
available from the British Library.

ISBN 978 1 80016 705 6

*Vanguard Press is an imprint of
Pegasus Elliot Mackenzie Publishers Ltd.*
www.pegasuspublishers.com

This is a work of fiction. Names, characters, businesses, places, events and
incidents are either the product of the author's imagination or used in a
fictitious manner. Any resemblance to actual persons, living or dead, or
actual events is purely coincidental

First Published in **2024**

**Vanguard Press
Sheraton House Castle Park
Cambridge England**

Printed & Bound in Great Britain

Dedication

To James Swan

Acknowledgements

Quotation taken from Damon Runyon's *Take It Easy*, page 34 line 26 to page 35 line 10."

Part One

Chapter 1

Franklin sat in his favourite chair near the window one calm and pleasant Sunday afternoon. The tumbler in his hand contained whiskey and water in an exact ratio of 6:1. In some things, Franklin was deeply precise. Darker into the room were Ruth, who lived with him, a couple of pals named Jem and Buster, and Buster's wife, Kitty.

The conversation was slow and desultory until Jem raised the paper he was looking at and called out, "Listen to this: 'Poltergeist activity is on the rise. From thirty-two reported incidents last year, this year already there are eighty-one. In Haddington alone there were eleven, and a police spokesman said that three of these were very serious.' What a caper, eh? That's eight poltergeist incidents that the police say were not very serious. That's hilarious."

The subject of poltergeists was examined with no great understanding or conviction. It might have passed on safely altogether had not Ruth declared that she had some experience of the phenomenon.

"I was at a séance once. My pal, Joyce, had just lost the aunty who had brung her up from childhood. She'd heard about communicating with the dead, and she begged me to come along. After a lot of rustling and mumbling, the medium told Joyce that her aunt was probably not long enough dead for contact to be possible. No joy for Joyce, unfortunately, but I did see the medium make a wee table rise off the floor and sort of shimmy though the air for a few feet before bumping down again."

The company added their opinions regarding that experience, all except Franklin, who, until then, had contributed nothing. The company felt very relaxed. Now he spoke.

"Furniture does not move unless somebody moves it. Anybody can use wires and strings to pretend to lift a little table. But what about this armchair of mine? Could a ghost move it? I'll challenge any ghost – living or dead." And then he got hold of the armchair by its back, slid one hand underneath its side and lifted it. He took three steps towards the window and sent the chair smashing through the glass and out and down to the street below.

"That's how you move furniture, folks."

He paused, aware of the horror on their faces in the dimness and looked behind him. He saw that he had no chair to sit on. He moved to the dark side of the room, and Jem stood up to offer Franklin his chair. Franklin walked past him and on into the kitchen, remarking, "Time for a refill."

A few minutes later, they heard him go out. Buster moved to where the window had been, looked down and saw what happened next. Franklin appeared on the pavement, stooped beside the chair and used a lighter to set fire to it. When its front was alight, he smothered the flames with his arms and then, when satisfied that the flames were out, left it blackened along the front and seat but otherwise, as it landed. The chair gazed up in astonishment at the face of Buster.

Buster described what he had seen.

Jem said, "Ruth, I'm starting to think the worst again. D'ye not agree? This is scary. It just does not seem to bother him."

Kitty leaned over and looked down. "There's two boys down there, looking at it. Were they there when it landed? Could've killed one of them. D'ye think they were there? Did you see them, Buster?"

"Ah was just looking at what Frankie was doing. They might've been there; I couldn't say."

Jem said he would go and get some plywood he had in his garage, which would keep out the draught – at least until they got the window fixed. Buster reminded Kitty that they had a rehearsal at three and would have to get moving. They all gave Ruth a hug and lame assurances that everything would be ok. They did not mention Franklin directly, having been through this sort of mayhem many times before.

Fortunately, it was spring, and the air was quite mild. Ruth made herself a cup of coffee and settled down to watch the latest episode of a serial she'd been recording. It was Norwegian and subtitled, and she kept losing the place, her mind wandering all the time. She pressed the pause button, closed her eyes and tried to think clearly. An armchair through the window and nobody is shocked. And sadly, this latest was not the worst case of Franklin's wildness. It was certainly ranked below the episode of the Chinese waiter – still missing – and well below any number of others. She was getting closer to the obvious decision – to walk away from here. Of course, even that move, if she ever summoned up the courage to make it, would not put her out of his reach. She had a sister in London. Frankie would reach her. She had cousins in Canada. Frankie would find her. He would give her some lovely present, beg forgiveness and assure her his mind was clean and whole. Down into a bottom corner of her mind crept the thought, all fizzing and excited, that it was not her who had to go – it was Franklin. Go how far? As far as it took.

The idea, now a little settled, began to expand and present a range of images of how the going of Franklin might be effected. The means chosen would have to be watertight, for there would be no second chance.

Her thoughts were broken by a bang and clatter at the front door, and there was Jem, struggling with a large sheet of plywood.

"No answer from the glaziers. But I got this. It'll keep out the wind until tomorrow. I'll just get it in place."

When he put the wood in place, the entire room fell into darkness. Ruth put on some lights. They stared at each other, each wondering if the other was at journey's end, when the door opened and Franklin stood there, holding a shopping bag and nodding in approval at Jem's handiwork.

"Good job, Jem, good job. Terrific – gives the place more atmosphere. Don't know if I prefer it without windows. Ha-ha – only joking."

Jem remained stony.

"Here's the glazier's number. If you get him early in the morning, he'll likely do the repair tomorrow."

"Thing is, Jem, I may have some other appointments early tomorrow. Have an early rise. And Ruth, of course, will be away and out working. Jem, d'ye think you could sort it for us? You're great at that. Where would we be without you, Jem? You phone, and maybe you could arrange to be here when he comes. Will mean a lot to me, Jem. You're my right-hand man. And you've got a key, eh? So you can pick your time. And help yourself, of course – food, booze – it's all yours."

Jem exchanged a glance with Ruth and bid farewell through closed lips.

Franklin came over and put his hands on Ruth's shoulders. She flinched but turned to look at his eyes. In an effort to relax, she breathed out, sighed and closed her hurting eyes.

"Listen, pet, you look a bit tired. When I was out, I picked up something nice for dinner. You'll love it. You sit down and rest. Watch some TV. I'll sort the dinner."

A moment later, he came in with a glass of cold white wine and offered it to her.

"There you are pet. A little prosecco has great healing properties."

How would you know? she thought. *You've never tried it.*

Ruth had three glasses before dinner was ready, but even then, she remembered to look at his eyes. Nothing to see. She was eating with gusto the fillet steak he had brought, feeling a little more relaxed, and they were chatting, some of the tension lifted.

Franklin asked, "Listen, Ruthie, do you know any bald women?"

"Sorry, Franklin, I think I must have misheard you there. What was that you said?"

"I asked whether you know any bald women."

"I've known one or two whose hair fell out with chemo treatment. Is that what you mean.?"

"Yes, that would do. But ideally, I meant women who chose to be bald – and to go around bald; not cover up with a wig."

"I remember that Irish singer, Sinead O'Connor, decided to go bald at one point, and it caused a bit of a stir. Remember her?"

"I thought her singing improved when she got rid of the hair."

"I have no doubt you have some reason for talking about this, Franklin, but I'll wait for you to tell me what it is."

Just then, Franklin's phone sounded, and he went out to take the call. Looking around, Ruth caught sight of the Tesco receipt on the sideboard. She examined it – the date on it was correct. And she saw only one item: a bottle of Johnny Walker Black Label. No steaks. No wine.

Franklin came back in. "Police. They spoke to me earlier. And now they'd like me to come over to the station. Within two hours, if possible. We'll finish this first, eh? No wasting good food – the best of food – just so a cop can tick his boxes and file his report."

"What did you say to them, Frankie? If I don't know what you said, we could get into trouble. We should get our story together, you know."

"I just told them the truth. It'll be okay. Nobody died."

"I'll come with you. Give me a few minutes to get ready. Call a taxi. The police station is one place you shouldn't drive to when you've been drinking."

"That was coke I was drinking."

"Coke and what? Brandy or whiskey? Frankie, please, today has been quite bad enough. Let's get through this last bit unscathed."

"We'll be all right. You worry too much."

They walked to the station, less than a mile away, and they were shown into a waiting room and joined almost immediately by two detectives. The taller one holding a file got started right away. The other, a woman wearing a wig, looked at them the whole time.

"Mr Gaddarini, I am going to read out your account of the incident earlier today. I will ask you to confirm it. The statement is,

'I was relaxing with a few friends and decided to light some scented house candles. I found a taper, lit it and was lighting the candles when I was distracted by the conversation. I realised the burning taper had fallen onto the armchair and set it alight. Thinking only of the safety of my friends, I somehow lifted the chair and managed to hurl it out the window. I then went down to check that it was no longer alight. When I saw it was safe and no one had got hurt, I went off to have a drink at the *Ewe and Lamb*. I was shaken and needed a drink to calm my nerves.'"

"Yes, that's about it."

"Miss Walsh, do you believe that statement matches your own? The mention of accidentally setting the chair on fire comes from Mr Gaddarini. There were some scorch marks on the chair, but our forensic people have already determined that those marks were produced after the chair fell and not before. And with the presence of some residue that is the result of an ordinary cigarette lighter, it is unlikely the flames were caused by any taper."

"I was sitting over by the table, furthest from Franklin. I was paying attention to a discussion we were having about poltergeists. The fire could have started without me seeing."

"Can one of you write down on this form the name and contact details of anyone else in the flat at the time of the incident? A report will be sent to the PF. If a charge of reckless endangerment is to be brought, you will be informed."

They stood up and showed Franklin and Ruth to the door.

Walking home, Ruth felt all the tension flood back.

"What on earth was that, Frankie? We don't have any scented candles – you threw out the last of them. What are the chances Jem or Buster or Kitty are going to mention bloody scented candles?"

"You must think quick at times. Be quick on your feet. It'll not be a problem. Listen, d'ye fancy a pint before bedtime?"

"I do not, Frankie. I'm half-drunk as it is."

"See ya later, pet," said Franklin, as he split and headed over to the *Ewe and Lamb*.

Chapter 2

Notoriously, Monday was such a quiet day in most barbershops that many did not open at all that day. They were often overworked on Saturdays and then took their weekend differently from everyone else.. Perhaps this was one factor in making barbers different.

Monday afternoon, Buster and Jem were drinking coffee and kept returning to the main topic: yesterday's launch of the armchair, and the remarkably close brush with death it brought to two youngsters.

"To me," said Buster," it summed up everything about him. Above everything else, he is impulsive. All the scrapes he's been in – and worse than scrapes – there was some trigger. And it came from a sudden impulse. He can almost never account for his bout of wild behaviour. Ye've just got to be ready and be prepared for anything when he's around. As far as ye can."

"D'you ever feel a bit like me; that he's getting too much to bear? Years ago he would be sorry and apologetic and try to make up for whatever mayhem he had caused. If I remember rightly, he got psychiatric treatment after he took away those dogs from Mrs Reid and painted them. Remember?"

"I go back a bit further. I remember a time when he seemed perfectly normal. When none of these things ever erupted like they do now. He admitted to me that he knew he was more and more acting out of character. He admitted it sometimes seemed out of his control. But he insisted psychiatry was nothing to do with what was happening to him. So he didn't stay the course with that treatment. Just laid low for quite a while."

"He'll be here any minute. Says he'll spell me while I let the glaziers in to do their work. I don't even know why he can't just be there. I'm running out of patience, pal or not."

True to form, Franklin strolled in, arms outstretched to give his mates a big, communal hug. It was not easy, given the Laurel-and-Hardy dimensions of his friends.

"Ok, Jem. Ah'm just passing through, in case ye were a bit puzzled. On my way to a meetin' with some medical committee who think I could be doing more to get back into work. Just saying hello."

"Ok, Frankie", said Jem, "I'll get over there and see the job done. Have the glaziers been paid?"

"Oh, aye, that's sorted. No problem. Great. See you later, Jem."

"Ok, Buster. I should be back before five."

Frankie picked up some scissors and started snipping away at the air.

"Ye know, Buster, I should have a try at this hair-cutting game."

"It's not as easy as you might think."

"Oh, come on. If Jem can cut hair, then so can anybody."

"You're wrong there, Frankie. Jem is a good, careful barber who rarely makes mistakes. I haven't had one complaint about him."

"What kinds of haircuts are you asked for, Buster? Same old?"

"Older guys it's mostly a tidy-up; a trim. But with youngsters, it can be a lot of things – purple Mohicans, Number One…"

"Number One – is that down to the bone? Yeah. Do much shaving? Or is that well out of date?"

"Not much. Punters are a little scared of the sight of a bare razor. Very sharp. Hard to keep blood off the floor."

"Eh? You're kidding, you swine. Though speaking of that, there are barbers down the Gallowgate quite familiar with blood. One of them has pouches of blood plasma hung from the ceiling, ready to replace any accidental slip. Ha-ha. No, that's a joke. But another barber down there, Big Billy, owner of *Big Billy's Aff Yer Heid*, has his own way of working. Billy gets juiced every Friday night, and so Saturday – very busy in the shop – he has trouble controlling the shakes enough to keep the punter in the chair safe from bloodletting. Billy has three chairs, and so on Saturdays he hires them out – sixty quid and the chair's yours for the rest of the day, and you keep your takings. He calls these helps his apprentices and doesn't look too closely at their credentials. I believe there's trouble every week. That East End – it's a madhouse. I bet you're glad to have a shop in such a nice neighbourhood."

Buster brought over two coffees and agreed. "It's probably the best area in Glasgow. No vandals, no street-brawls; no potholes even."

"Quite. But looking again at your pricelist here, Buster, don't you think you're just about giving things away? I mean, you're so cheap."

"Part of our appeal and our family name –Ma was never expensive."

"It's a different age, Buster. You got to make a living. You could nearly double those prices. Especially with the quality of service you provide."

"You being funny again, Frankie?"

"No, no. If you put about 40% on your prices across the board, soon you could even move into this neighbourhood."

"No thanks, Frankie."

"You wouldn't want me as your neighbour, eh? That what you're thinking? Heh-heh. God, it's quiet, Buster."

"Aye, but ye always get a few in. Anyway, if I didn't open, she'd hear about it right away, no question."

"The mother? How is she?"

"Well, they can't operate. They give her a year at most. They advised her to get a routine into her day. So her routine is to drink no gin until five p.m. and then to drink only gin after five p.m. She calls it a balanced life. She still thinks she's funny. Auld witch. Another one of her ideas of a joke is to tease me about inheriting this place – or not. It was hers to start with, of course, as I've told you – a ladies hairdressers. She passed it on to me to work as a gents' barbers. But she's still the owner."

"Well, Buster, it's sure to come to you next year, or whenever. Have you been thinking of bringing that day forward, by some manner of means?"

"No, I have not. She's a bad old crone, but she is my mother. Don't you have one?"

"I do – or I did. Haven't seen her since the wedding, so she may be gone. What about Kitty? I mean, what does she think of your ma?"

"She just plays it cool and safe and advises me to do the same. Kitty did remark on something I've noticed myself."

"What was that?"

"My mother is quite fond of Jem. She asks after him a lot. She likes chatting to him on the phone, and she regularly reminds me of what a reliable worker he is."

"So? So she's crazy."

"No, but I just have this feeling she might be generous to Jem in her will. I know what she's thinking."

"No! That's ridiculous. You can easily put her off. Tell her he's started to come in late for work Or, if necessary, tell her Jem's a paedophile."

"What!?"

"If you need to do something, then you need to do it."

"Right, Frankie, time to go. Haven't you a meeting to get to?"

"No, I was just kidding. The meeting's next week. I think."

As Frankie stood up to leave, a customer came in. While Buster showed him to a seat, Franklin lifted a comb and scissors from beside a sink and left.

Chapter 3

It was still referred to by many as the new graveyard, but it had been opened one hundred and sixty years earlier when the nearest cemetery reached capacity. Despite the city council's insistence that it was democratic in all matters relating to burials, the new graveyard, from the beginning had been the terminus only for affluent citizens, and for all purposes was a private cemetery. No riffraff got into these graves, and the tombs themselves spoke loudly of wealth and worth. No 'Karens' or 'Jimmys'; no 'McGraws' or 'McTavishes'. The gold names on the tombstones declared their occupants to be 'Lady Rowena di Fargo', not far from the solid marble of 'Baron Vergenstein', below whose name was the appeal 'Be tender with your memory' and below that, 'Misunderstood'. Not all the occupants were from the nobility. Tarpaulin the Swimmer, for whom the tombstone claimed, 'He swam till he drowned', might have been from any rank of society. Several rows along, there was a 'Morella' and an 'Ariel'. Above one grave the stone was in pyramid shape, and the inscription was in some ancient tongue. *Occult, perhaps,* thought Franklin. And next to it was a stone with fiend-like gargoyles at each corner, their eyes bulging and their tongues snaking out.

Before he knew what he was doing, Franklin started to imagine the sort of sounds such creatures would make. He shocked himself by producing, simultaneously, a hissing sound and a sort of gurgle. They wound in and out of each other in a weird symphony, but when he tried to repeat it a moment later, he found it impossible. For a few seconds, his throat was intensely painful. Then it faded and passed.

Its official name was 'The Levels', again suitably odd, because it had been sculpted into the side of a hill, and the layers ran in terraces around the curve of that hill. Spotless, grass cut, shrubbery exquisite in choice and placing, it probably never in its one hundred and sixty odd years had a single complaint.

Franklin used his electronic pass to open the graveyard gate and walked in. He liked it here. After strolling around for about fifteen minutes reading the monuments, he headed towards his favourite. Fairly high up the hill, there was a granite tombstone on which was written THE LONE GLASWEGIAN. Below this was engraved, 'He was very rich when he died, but when he sank to his grave he was again as poor as when he was born in Glasgow'.

Again, Franklin paused here and stood in thought. He found this stone drew him powerfully but still could not explain to himself why. He glanced at his watch and saw he was almost late.

On the other side of the hill from The Levels, sat a lovely housing estate, rather proud of its status and old grandeur, and smug in its assumption that only the best lived there. It might be called, today, an exclusive estate. Franklin lived in a desirable estate, but not an exclusive one, which is why he always approached here in a respectful manner. His destination was a house known rather jarringly as The Resting Place. It had CCTV and a controlled gate. Franklin buzzed and drove in across the crunchy, wheaten stones between the bougainvillea and stopped in the small parking area to the side of the mansion.

He walked round to the front entrance and was greeted by Tam, one of the place's Jack-of-all-trades. He was struck anew by the facial resemblance between Tam and the late, great Bela Lugosi. Yet he was a twenty-eight-year-old dancer. Franklin had assumed that like other Scottish Tams, his true name was Tom or Thomas. But no – on an earlier visit his host had explained that the man insisted his name was Tamburlaine, and they had come to an agreement that while he was in situ or working in Mr Patrick's employ, he would be known as Tam.

His voice was fluty and pleasant. "Mr Gaddarini! Hello! You are expected." In a lower voice, he added, "He's in a very good mood. So there. You know where to go."

Franklin turned second left off the hallway into a bright sitting room, with couches and divans facing every which way. A sturdy, round table, almost glowing in its whiteness, helped indicate the room's latitude and longitude. Music was playing quietly – perhaps some Benedictine chant from medieval times.

An old man sat in a far corner on a deep-green couch. He was elegantly dressed – a three-piece suit, tie and brogues – and was holding a notebook. At the sight of Franklin, he rose and welcomed him. Franklin approached, as ever awestruck by the unaged complexion before him. This man looked about fifty. Yet he was closer to eighty.

"Nice to see you, Franklin. You look a little tired if I may say so. Not overworking, are you? "

"No, no, Mr Patrick, it's just the cares that come with living in our time. Stress, stress, stress."

"Oh – so glad I missed that, then. I am older, you know. Did you come straight here, or did you go round to the tombs first?"

"I came straight here. I felt I was a little late."

"Well, don't neglect the tombs. Think how privileged they are. Think of your own motherland where they bury people in boxes in the wall, with a key to come and open them and have a chat! Spare us all that. We do things better here, Franklin. Your poor father – where is he interred?"

"I've no idea, Mr Patrick. I lost trace of him."

"So sad, Franklin; so many sad breaks in continuity. What's to become of us at all? So you've lost touch with him. I knew him, did you know that? Yes, years ago we were sort of co-workers in an interesting enterprise. And your mother. I remember you telling me you hadn't seen her for years."

"That's right. Since my wedding."

"Franklin, you're all adrift. Your journey must be difficult. Your mother, now; I knew her a little, you know."

"You did? I had no idea."

"Do you have a photo of her?"

"A photo? Probably have one somewhere."

"Could you get a photo of your mother for me?"

"I will try. There are a lot of places I could try. I'll let you know."

"Thanks, Franklin. Now listen. We're having tea soon, and Mr Mick is coming over. You've met him. Mr Angelo sends apologies – he has a bad cold. But before that, I was wondering if you would read to me again, like the last time. Even with my glasses, I struggle now to read for any length of time. That young chap who comes over on some Thursdays, he was the last to read. Here's the book – it's one by Damon Runyon; one of his stories. The page where he stopped is marked; I think it was called Cemetery Bait. What a title! Yes, go ahead.

Franklin took a moment and then started reading. "'While I am waiting in the nightclub for Tommy Entrata, I observe, at another table, the most beautiful Judy I see in many a day. She is young and has hair the colour of straw, and she is dressed in a gorgeous, white evening gown, and she has plenty of junk on her in the way of diamonds. I am so impressed by her that I call Emil, the headwaiter, and question him, because Emil is an old friend of mine, and I know he always has a fund of information on matters such as this.

'Emil,' I say, 'Who is the lovely pancake over there by the window?'

'Cemetery bait,' Emil says, so I know she is married and has a husband who is selfish about her, and naturally, I cast no sheep's eyes in her direction.'"

He had read for about twenty minutes when Tam appeared, seemingly out of the carpet beneath him, and announced the presence of Mr Mick, friend and confidant of Mr Patrick. Franklin stopped and put the book down.

Mick bowed, shook his hand and said, "I love a good comedy. A good laugh, ye know? This life is so full of woe and catastrophe. That sounded like a modern comedy, from the little I overheard."

"Pay no attention to him, Franklin. He makes jokes where he shouldn't. Especially with great works of literature, which he himself knows well and thoroughly."

Tam reappeared, pushing a tall trolley loaded with food and tea. He placed a legged tray on the lap of each man, sorted the sandwiches and cakes where they would be accessible, and placed on each, crockery and a teapot. Franklin had been in this room several times before but never for tea. He had assumed they would take it from the big, round table, but obviously this was kept for grander things.

He tried and savoured a long, slightly crispy roll carrying smoked trout with pesto and some herbs and found it one of the best things he had ever eaten. Patrick saw this and chuckled with pleasure. The three men gathered around and ate and drank with great contentment. They talked about football, their favourite beers and other odd things.

Pouring their second cups, Mr Mick remarked, "I hear there was an incident round your way yesterday, Frank. Police involved. Did you hear anything of that?"

Franklin's motto 'be quick on your feet' was being tested.

"It could be called an incident. It could have been much more than an incident. What happened was, I was lighting some candles, when somehow a spark dropped onto an armchair. I turned away, talking to somebody, and when I looked back, the chair was on fire. I supposed I erred on the side of panic rather than coolness, but I lifted the whole chair and threw it through the window. I don't know where |I got the strength. It was a big, solid, old-fashioned chair. Thankfully, nobody was down below at the time. I suppose that's what you were referring to, Mr Mick?"

"No, no, not at all. Armchairs? Flung out of a window? God, that place is getting worse. Patrick, maybe you should see about a new residence for Franklin here."

"Well, what are you talking about, Mick? Apart from the armchair, it was just a quiet Sunday."

"I've been told that two young boys were passing by. They'll have told their parents. They will maybe go to the police."

"Have the police been in touch?" asked Patrick.

"Yes, but about the armchair, not about any youngsters."

"So, you launched an armchair into orbit just minutes before two young boys walked by. They could be dead by now, and you could be in terrible trouble, and we might get investigated. Can I just remind you that the dealings we have, you and I, run smoothly without any outside curiosity. We go about our business, we hurt no one, and we help people. But all of this is not necessarily understood by those outside our group – our company. And especially do we not wish to attract any attention from the police. I'm sure you get the message. And of course, it's also very much in your interest. I know you'll keep me informed of any pertinent developments. So, having said that, let's turn to some much more pleasant matters. Mick here has a friend who is interested in joining us. That would bring our number above thirty, and that is getting a little too high for my liking. Anyway, Mick's new friend, George, is keen to come along a week from tomorrow. Could you have something – I mean someone – for us?"

He took a moment to check Franklin over. Six feet tall, lean and lithe, with much athletic potential that he had never used, yet remained almost slim. His hair was black, thick and rich-looking, and his brown eyes had a startling depth that belied the lack of substance behind them. The Roman nose suggested a nobility somewhere in his pedigree, though it had never yet been traced, and it overhung a long mouth that rarely smiled and rarely scowled. He bore a three-inch scar just below his left jawline as a magnet to attract ladies. He was a born winner. And once he had done the attracting and passed them on to the care of Patrick and his merry band, his work was done. Patrick fully retained confidence in his wayward protégé.

`I could, Mr Patrick. Closer to the time you'll send me the numbers required, and I'll see that all runs smoothly. There will be one new addition. I'll get the details to you."

"Please do. I'm fond of surprises, but I also like the joys of anticipation. Do you have your notebook there? Yes. Now, could you check if sixty-seven and seventy-three are available soon. It's just that I've had a special request."

Franklin took out a tablet from an inside pocket of his coat and fussed around for a minute.

"Seventy-three is available – and keen. Sixty-seven is no longer available – has left the country. Which means I would have to run a tutorial and then a pre-appearance check with seventy-three. Can you OK that, please?"

"Certainly, I can. Lovely. That's us up and running. Mick, is all well with you?"

"Well, Mr Patrick, if there's one thing that keeps me up and running, it's this place of yours. You're a lucky man."

"I am, but I think it not boastful to claim that I have shaped a lot of that luck by my own thinking. Now, time for one of my TV programmes. So I'll bid you both good evening. Tam is busy, so please see yourselves out."

Just as he was getting into his car, Franklin paused and looked to his left. Sure enough, there was the top end of the graveyard. It swept right round the hillside and ran right up to the fence, which was the boundary with grounds of *The Resting Place*.

Chapter 4

Beth pulled into her garage, almost afraid to look up and see whether the window had been replaced. She kept her head down until she was inside the house, then looked and sighed with much relief; to which she immediately added a glass of red wine. She examined the window frame and approved the work. No sign of Franklin, but that was no surprise. One day it was wine and steaks, then off the planet for two or three days.

She worked in a medical centre as a receptionist and had always run her life wisely and quietly. Then she had started to think that Franklin might be the partner she was looking for. So they had hooked up, and after eight months, the leaves were losing some of the greenery. The room looked wounded with one side of the couch no longer nestling against its left armchair. But before giving thought to that, Ruth knew it was time to give her sister, Betsy, a call.

She hadn't really caught Franklin on the rebound, as some people liked to put it. He and Agnes had been separated for about eight years when Ruth finally succeeded in getting him to notice her. It had happened one Friday night at the *Ewe and Lamb*, where she and two pals landed at a table adjacent to Franklin who was in a heated conversation with an Eastern gentleman. Once the glances and the looks had got into a rhythm, it somehow just seemed certain that they would speak. They arranged to meet at the same place the following night. Two weeks later, she had cancelled the lease for her little rental flat and had moved into Franklin's spacious apartment, a split-level affair that made it seem more like a house than a flat.

His advice had been, "Say you're my housekeeper. That's nice and vague and saves a lot of embarrassment and confusion."

That had been disappointing, but she had accepted it, reflecting that she was not his lover, friend, companion, partner or mistress, but little segments of all of them. There were bigger disappointments, and they came from totally new and unexpected incidents and revelations. For example, out of the blue, she learned that Franklin worked as a TEFL tutor in a local college, teaching English to Italians and Spaniards. She saw no outward signs of such work – no files, briefcase or textbooks. She tried to talk about the subject. He did not welcome any curiosity. He said everything nowadays was done online. He also hinted that he was tired of the job and would be packing it in at the end of June. So she kept her curiosity to herself.

Franklin had met her parents and seemed to impress her mother, who told Ruth she had a smouldering Latino there. Maybe she would have changed her description now that the Latino was setting armchairs alight and firing them like mediaeval weapons. Ruth's father was polite and courteous at the meeting, but Ruth could see that he was not convinced. Since then, five months before, Franklin had not had any meetings with the Swifts.

Ruth had this gnawing idea that talking to Betsy would not be beneficial to her future with Franklin if there was to be one. Betsy was tough and direct and spoke her feelings through thinned lips and narrowed eyes.

She phoned. Betsy answered immediately and took Ruth aback right away. She suggested they meet in a pew in the back of St John's Church. Betsy said it would be open because a body was being brought in later for a funeral the next morning. Ruth agreed. She scribbled a note for Franklin to tell him where she was. Then she paused, scrunched it up and put it in her pocket. She was going to stop telling him everything.

Just as she was ready to leave, she paused for a moment. There was a short staircase up to the bedrooms, and just before the top, a little passage sloped up to the left, to what Franklin described as his den. Ruth had never been inside. Now, emboldened by the wine, she went up and looked around the small room. A desk took up most of the space. She opened the bottom right-hand drawer and saw eight opened boxes of Priadel – opened and empty. So he was taking them. That worried her. The bottom left-hand drawer contained an altar boy's medal with attached red cord, and a little book called *The Altar Boy's Handbook.* Her head began to swim, and she quickly retreated out of the room, out of the house, and walked the quarter mile to St John's.

The musty, incense-heavy air of the old church had a calming effect on Ruth, as she slipped into the pew beside her sister.

"I know. It's mad – a church. But we'll have peace and not be disturbed here."

"Wouldn't the café have been just as good?"

"No. Because Frankie is sure to look in there. He'd know that's where we'd be. He will not come into the chapel. No way."

"What do you mean? How do you know that?"

"He hates religion. No that's not true. He's scared of religion. Remember that funeral we were at back in September? I heard him talking to people there. He's afraid of God. The God, that is, that he says doesn't exist. He doesn't exist, but Frankie's afraid of him. Anything holy, he keeps away."

Ruth thought of the altar boy stuff she had just discovered but said nothing.

"Betsy, I am really beginning to wonder about what I'm doing with him. Listen to this."

Ruth described the events of the armchair in detail, as well as the police interest and Frankie's total lack of interest.

"I know it's a cliché, but I told you from the start to be ultra-careful with that madman. And now? Who throws a chair out of a window? And he's on lithium; supposed to stabilise him."

"I found eight empty packets, so I assume he's taking them. But if he is, it's even more serious, because he is as erratic as ever. And why he would he keep all the boxes, in a drawer?"

"Probably he's opening the boxes, throwing away the pills and keeping the boxes, to fool you. That is dangerous. Ruth, it's time to get outta there. What about sex? That still going?"

"Sort of. You could say it's regular but not frequent. And it's…"

"What?"

"It's got to have a particular flavour; a particular style."

"Flavour? What the hell? You mean like raspberry ripple?"

Ruth paused and looked around the dim house of God. There was nobody present. And they had plenty of time. It was hard to express this, but she would give it a try.

"Most people, me included, see Franklin as a bit of a macho man. So I was a little wary the first time. It was going well enough, and then he just stopped. Couldn't keep it hard. Just gave up. I said not to worry. Three nights later, we snuggled up again. Same result – he couldn't keep his dick hard. I was apprehensive, thinking he might get angry; might take it out on me. But the next time, he asked would I mind trying something a bit different. Christ, he's going to tie me up! I thought. But no. He just went to sleep. I decided to let him sort it out in his own good time. A week later, we were in the kitchen. He started a little smooching, but I could see he was nervous. He suggested a little game he'd like us to play, later, when we were in bed. He would be the great magician – Magaloo or something. I was the eastern maiden, Potrella. Magaloo would save me from the great serpent, Tangwa. Potrella would show her deep gratitude by giving herself, body and soul, to Magaloo. I had to bite down to not treat it comically, in case Magaloo went berserk. And it worked – for both of us. The relief was almost as big as the orgasm. We go for it about once a fortnight, and that seems about right. He suggested another game as a change, but it didn't work. Something to do with a lion and a gazelle, from some Greek myth, but it quickly got abandoned. I think he didn't really get the story right on that one. I don't think he knows what a gazelle is. We haven't been doing it so much recently, but when we do, I must remember I'm Potrella and act accordingly."

"And you don't think this guy is wacky?"

"It's not that unusual – a bit of fantasy. It's known as role-play."

"Just remind me what chapter of the catechism role-play is mentioned."

They were silent for a little spell.

Betsy had an idea. "Fancy we go down and light a candle?"

"What for?"

"You remember how when we were little, we loved it at the end of Mass when Mammy gave us a coin each to go down and light a candle? It's a symbol – the light fights off the darkness. And Ruthie, babe, there is a lot of darkness coming up around you."

They went down, lit a candle each and stood in silence. Betsy shut her eyes and muttered intensely some prayer from of old. Ruth felt quite at peace, but her mind stayed vacant.

Back in the rear pew, she confided, "I never know what to make of God."

"Show me somebody who does," whispered Betsy in reply.

A door clanked open behind them, and an old priest came in, gave them a wave and tottered up the centre aisle to the altar where he fussed around. Aware that the funeral party might be arriving soon, the sisters agreed to leave.

On the steps outside, Betsy said, "Fancy a drink?"

"I haven't even eaten anything yet."

"Fine. Let's share a steak pie over at *The Palace* and get a couple of gins into us."

The mood in *The Palace* was as ever confident, but not brash, and the sisters soon relaxed, reminisced and confided ridiculous ideas to each other. The main idea which kept rising to the surface was expressed thus by Betsy, just before she started on her fourth gin.

"You'll need to leave him or suffer. And he's not worth suffering for."

Ruth tried to convey how it was not as straightforward as that; that there were puzzles and mysteries about Franklin that were fascinating, even though they might involve danger. Her efforts to tell her sister that her life had not had enough danger came to little.

"Our Rob is going to Uni in September. I'll have a spare room. Come and stay with me and Brendan. It'll be great. To hell with Franklin the Magnificent, or whatever."

"You're so sweet to me, Betsy. But for a start, this is only March, and who knows how many small pieces he'll have chopped me into by September."

"Oh, Jesus, Ruthie, don't talk like that. There'll be no chopping done. You said something back there that made more sense. It's not you that'll have to go. He'll have to go."

Both women were aware that they were speaking recklessly and through drink, but they also knew that that was what drink was for. Ruth remembered yesterday's meal with Franklin and told Betsy about the store receipt that showed no payment for wine or steak.

"Why would he steal them, Betsy? Why shoplift when he has plenty of money?"

"Plenty of money. That surprises me."

"Well, me too. I mean his salary as a college lecturer will be good, but it hardly puts us in the luxury class."

"College lecturer? Frankie?"

"Yes. He lectures in the Foreign Languages section in Anniesland College."

"I just don't believe that, honey. Frankie is not an academic. How'd you think he was? Did he tell you himself?"

"He's mentioned it briefly once or twice, although he never really wants to talk about it; I've noticed that."

"I wonder why. He's a lying bastard, Ruthy. You must get him out of your life."

"No, no, Betsy. He'd never be able to run a lie, a pretence, as big as that."

"Men invented frauds. You've no evidence he is what he says. Best way to find out is to phone Anniesland College, say you're the sister of Mr Gaddarini in the TEFL department, and ask to speak to him. See what happens."

The Palace was the bar where both sisters had been weaned into the Glasgow social life. It was where they felt they belonged, and so the sessions stretched on and on, as they caught up with events and people. Finally, a taxi dropped off each in turn at their home.

Chapter 5

Somebody was talking. Talking to who? Ruth turned onto her back and listened. People were talking. For the second time that morning, she waited till the fog cleared. The first time, ages before, she had woken up with such a hangover that she had to call in to work and say she would be in by lunchtime. Now maybe it was mid-morning. She rose and drank a pint of water and then went into the hallway. The living room door was ajar, and through the crack, she could see Franklin and a woman standing talking. She was well-dressed and had a pleasant face. She would be in her forties. Ruth held her breath and tuned in.

"... In December. But that was exceptional. A Christmas bonus, you could call it. It'll still be well worth your while."

"But I need to know how much. I have a right to that. And I have a couple of other questions, especially about who will be there."

"Stop worrying, Bebette. Remember all those anxieties you had a year ago? Didn't think it could be done? Felt sure you were gonna be mistreated? But no. Were you?"

"No. Nor the next times, but December I kind of thought things changed a bit. I didn't feel as relaxed, as secure, as before."

"Bebette, I swear on my father's grave that you are in safe hands. It's not even what they used to call a floor show. It's just – a little, clean entertainment."

"I hope Lucille is down to go. I feel quite confident when she's there."

"I am just about to call her and confirm that. Two weeks ago she said yes, and I have no reason to think that'll have changed."

Ruth made a coughing sound and stepped into the room. She also realised that Franklin had not known she was in the house. He must have arrived since her call to the office. But he seized the situation silkily by the throat.

"Ah, there you are, pet. Having a lie-in? She works so hard, Bebette. I'm so glad that now and again she just gives in and collapses and really catches up on her sleep."

Ruth was baffled. Who was this? When had she come in? Where on earth had Franklin been? Why was he not at work, in the college? She planted herself in the solitary armchair and giggled a little at the thought of that armchair's mate crashing through the window. Whoever this woman was, she must be wondering why the room contained only two pieces of a three-piece suite. Ruth, still a little drunk, was dying to tell Bebette about the flying armchair.

She just smiled. "So, Bebette, are you at the college too?"

She saw that Bebette did not know what she was talking about. Again, Franklin scrambled to rescue the situation.

"No, Ruth, she isn't, but I got to know her through a connection with the college. Bebette's an entertainer, you see. She operates within a very specialised niche. Not at all well known. Not in the public eye, you might say."

Both women knew a lie when they heard one, and their glances crossed. Ruth felt a little regret that, mentally, she was not quite up to prolonging this inquisition.

"I need to take a shower," she said. "I'll leave you to discuss business." She went out of the room.

Bebette immediately stepped up. "I must go. I'm sorry."

"What? No, don't be silly. Everything's OK. I've still quite a few pieces of information to give you."

"I don't want to know. I've lost interest. And quite honestly, I can't trust you. Don't worry. I can keep quiet. Tell your friend thanks for the advance. And please take this as final. Do not contact me any further. Oh, and my friend Lucille? I'll be telling her about this. I don't think you'll be seeing her again, either."

She was gone. Franklin stood with his mouth hanging open. He started to pace around, muttering and cursing, then seemed to come to an important decision. He got his phone and called Mr Patrick.

"Hello, there, Mr P. Up early today. Had your porridge, I suppose."

He cringed as he realised how stupid he sounded. Porridge?

"What have you to tell me, Franklin?"

"I'm afraid there's been a bad turning. I think I've just lost number seventy-one. And, possibly, also number seventy-eight."

Mr Patrick asked him to repeat what he had said, and he did.

Mr Patrick said, "Just a minute while I get the book." He continued. "Ok, that is noted. But an explanation will be needed, as well as an insurance check. But not now; later, when we meet. I will contact you. Stay calm."

Franklin sat for a while, his mind elsewhere and his eyes blinking a lot. When Ruth came in dressed for work, he slipped automatically into appeasement mode, hoped everything was well with her. But she showed immediately that she was the third person in thirty minutes to be very displeased with Franklin. She had been thinking about her sister's advice and had called Anniesland College. They had no Gaddarini employed there.

"What is it you actually do over there at the college?" she asked him.

"You know. I told you. I'm a tutor in Teaching English as a Foreign Language to Italian and Spanish students."

"They've never heard of you. They have no Gaddarini on the books. You don't work there."

"Hang on, hang on. Of course I work there. Only not under my own name – Gaddarini. These Italian students who want to learn English want to be taught by someone who is British. They don't want an Italian teaching Italians, English. You get it? So, I gave a different name. I told them I was Ronnie. Ronnie McDonald."

"Jesus. You think I believe that? And did you add that your nickname was Big Mac? You expect me to believe that a further education college would not check up on your identity, especially now in the terrorist age we're living in? I'm going to work. And then tomorrow I'm seeing a lawyer to get some guidance about my rights. It would be better if you just took off for a while. I know it's in your name, the flat, but I'll get out of it as soon as possible. I won't wreck it. I won't throw any of your stuff through the window. But while I'm organising where I'm going next, I think you should be elsewhere. I'm supposed to end now with, 'See you in court', but I don't expect you'd turn up. Anyway, I do not want to see you at all."

"Ruth, just who have you been talking to? Somebody has been filling your head with a load of rubbish."

But the door closed firmly. For a while, he came and went around the flat, not deep in thought but trying to bring some cunning to bear on the various traps he was caught in and to find a way out – as he always had, he reminded himself. Ruth could wait – that was easy, although recalling her final words and tone gave him a chill. That police thing: that would be OK. Probably never hear another thing about it. Mr Patrick – now that was the problem.

Two years previously, the old man had taken great pains to explain his enterprise in detail to Franklin. He went over the details time and again. He emphasised the supremacy of security and confidentiality in this venture. Franklin and six others, perhaps including some women, were termed Scouts and Suppliers – that was their rank and position. They worked for a generous fee paid by Mr Patrick and his fellow members. Franklin had no idea how many of them there were. Bonuses were paid on two criteria – the recruitment of trustworthy entertainment, and the degree to which the actual entertainment matched the expectations of the members. Those who agreed to come and entertain were simply given a number.

When he had listened to all this stuff the first time, Franklin assumed it was just another prostitution racket, only more classy, less sordid and therefore acceptable. The whole playbook of the club told him otherwise. But he couldn't believe what they were saying –that no sexual contact was involved; that it was about the freedom to admire beauty without fear or shame. *OK, he thought. Maybe it is. Who cares? Where else would I get money like this?* He stuck to the job he was asked to do – scouting and recruiting. Feelings were too confusing, so he kept them limited to being a competent worker.

He got a text message from Mr Patrick asking him to call at *The Resting Place* the following day at three p.m. Franklin felt relief. He had a full day to construct a plausible story. He felt a little better and saw it was time for lunch.

It was Tuesday, midday, at the *Ewe and Lamb*. About half a dozen regulars were propped around and about the same number of visitors. Franklin went over and sat on a stool at the bar, as he preferred to do. He had hardly started into his burger when Diabolical Davie slipped onto the stool beside him.

"Well, Davie – you're early, are you not?"

"Time means nothing to me, Frankie. You should know that. I just spin around in time with the globe. And may I add, no offence, but you look as if you are very out of time with things. You look like about sixty percent of yourself. Maybe that burger will help. I doubt it. Junk food'll only make you worse and worse."

"Davie, if you're here to cheer me up, you've got off to a very poor start. I have a great deal that's slowing me down, at the minute. Weighted down by worries from all over. And I am not going to start describing all that. Tell you what, Davie, if you really want to help, go and play a song from the Jukebox with the track *Somebody* from the *Long Road out of Eden* album."

"Ok, but in case I forget – The Arab was in, looking for you. Something about a new job. Quite urgent. Said he'll catch you later."

"Thanks. If he came in here in the morning, it must be urgent. Usually, it's good news when The Arab himself is involved. Good pay-packet, you know?"

"It's up to you, but if you want to add to those worries that are weighing you down, The Arab's the go-to man."

A moment later, and The Eagles were spooking out with *Witchy Woman*.

"How's that, Frankie boy? You don't want some bright and breezy crooner thinking he can lift your spirits. No, you gotta get down and funky and drown in the trouble, then you'll come out of them stronger. Soon's I saw that title in the Jukebox – Bam! I knew it was the one for you."

Bam is the right word, thought Frankie. He did not know Davie well, and the little he did, always made him feel suspicious. He didn't know what of.

"I know you don't want to talk about the details. All that theory about talking out your troubles, especially to some psychiatrist, is a load of junk."

"I know it, Davie. Believe me. I've been there."

"You've done the psycho talk? Well. How did it feel? Any good?"

"He talked for three minutes. I talked for twenty-five minutes. Then he talked for two minutes. And that was it. Next, please. Every week for eight weeks. Although I never completed it. Week seven, I just thought, 'This is baloney. This bald guy says nothing to me, just sits there and hypnotises me with his paedo-like smile, daring me to stop talking.' So I packed it in. You're right – talking is no answer. Although, occasionally, you can be lucky, and you just collide with the right person at the right moment, and the talk turns out enjoyable and fruitful."

The Eagles song was just finishing, and Davie could not resist asking, "Bet there's somebody tangled up in your trouble, Frankie."

"Davie, don't make me knock you off that stool. No talking is no talking."

"OK, OK. You had your chance there, Frankie. And remember – all secrets are safe with me. And I believe I have a good idea for you, Frankie."

"Davie, your ideas are always worth considering. But right now, I need to focus on me a bit. I've got things that need quite a lot of attention. So, if you don't mind…"

"Best of luck with all that, Frankie. The tide comes in, and the tide goes out. I'll be seein' you."

Franklin turned to say something, but Davie was gone. *Strange bloke*, thought Franklin. *Maybe he would have given me some good advice.* He was known to be lucky. Once, he had been in big trouble on a burglary charge which involved a lot of jewellery. The case was simple. He was found guilty and remanded to Perth prison while awaiting sentence. His lawyer told him to expect eight years in jail. Then just before sentencing, there was an astonishing turn of events. The evidence had been mishandled, there was the possibility of police collusion, and the sentence was over-ruled. Davie told the story, quite humbly, to his pals in the *Ewe and Lamb* that night.

"I am lucky," he suggested. "My guardian angel is looking after me. Now buy me a whiskey, and you might get a share in my luck!"

Thus mused Franklin, wondering if it was only bad luck that had got him into this mess. After his second beer, he began to feel that he could take care of the home situation – a little of his well-honed flattery and sweetness would eventually melt Ruth back into the shape he liked her. He couldn't just go for a nice home-cooked dinner so soon. It would have to be something a bit more special. She liked the theatre. He could check what was on at *The Citizens* and go there and have a night out. He would have to suffer through some damned, modern drama he wouldn't understand. But that was a small price to pay. Yes, that might do it.

He knew a third pint was unwise at this time of day, but he got the idea that he would keep drinking until he had got a working plan for his worries, especially the forthcoming visit to Mr Patrick. There was a thin layer of sentiment involved in this. He did feel grateful to the old guy for trusting him and being very generous to him. He did like the degree of responsibility he had been given, and he liked to think he was relied on. But mostly, he liked the money that came with the work, and he dreaded to think of having to manage without those fees and bonuses.

Then, as if out of nowhere at all, a conviction came to him. He would have to get out of Glasgow for a while. He laughed to himself at the cliché of 'until the heat dies down', but the prospect had a lot of appeal. Like most messages that float in on a tide of alcohol, it should have caused him to be wary. But it never seemed to work like that. And right away came another conviction. He wondered why Mr Patrick had postponed their meeting until the next day. And a thought struck him that this was a ruse to make him feel secure for a day. Maybe in the meantime, right at that moment, even, someone was on the way to interview him. Hadn't he just heard the Eagles warning. "Somebody's following you"?

Yes, he would have to get moving. Franklin had a sudden lovely anticipation of being in Ireland again.

He made his way home and thought he would stop in and say hello at the barber shop. He got no further than the doorway, where Buster blocked his entry.

"What's up? You're not cutting hair, anymore? Come on, Buster. I want to speak—"

"You're not welcome here, Frankie. I can't let you in. I've had enough of you. And I speak for Jem. You lied about paying the glazier. He had to fork out cash for that job, which you assured him was already paid. That was worse than mean, Frankie. You're not poor."

"OK, OK, but you're making a big mistake. You've got it wrong."

Franklin was stepping away when he heard Buster call after him. "And I want that tortoiseshell comb and my Jaguar scissors returned pronto. I saw you pinch them yesterday. Give them to Ruth to give me back. I use them a lot. But you stay away."

Chapter 6

A google search told him there were seven ferry trips a day by Stena line between Cairnryan and Belfast. But first, he phoned his cousin, Tommy Jordan, whose house, just off Dublin's North Strand, was always open to relatives. Any family member was encouraged to visit and stay awhile. He was something of a lovable rogue, was Tommy, and love of family was not his only interest in life. He claimed to be acquainted with many of Dublin's good, bad and ugly. Franklin worked out it was eight or ten years since his last visit. Before that, the visits were much more frequent.

"Hello, there, Tom, you scallywag. How've ya been? Years since I've seen ya. Yes, listen. I have two weeks holiday right now, and I thought what better could I do than get over and sink a jar or two with Tom the Roving Boy. It's far too long since I've been over. I'm a disgrace, I know. That's if it suits, of course. Yes. No problem, Tommy. I'll book a ferry to Belfast tomorrow midday and be down in Dublin by the evening. Will I just come straight to yourself there or take a hotel for a night or two? Yes, yes, of course – no offence taken. Yes – just me. Honeymoon suite? Not necessary. Right. I'll see you soon. Phone you when I'm getting close. Lovely. Bye."

He phoned Stena and booked on for the sailing at noon the next day. He wouldn't drink any more tonight, so that he could have a clear head for the double-drive tomorrow. He took his passport, bank cards, cash, clothes and the usual toiletries. Once his case was packed, he paused and wondered. Shouldn't there be someone he needed to tell where he was going, or just that he was going and would be back in a while?

"Who will I tell?" He spoke aloud but got only an echo.

Sod them all, he snarled, and took his case down to the car. He was scarcely back up in the flat when he heard voices on the stairs. He checked his watch. Half past four. It couldn't be Ruth home from work yet. But it was, and with her came Betsy and Brendan.

A simple greeting of 'hello' would have sufficed. But Franklin's mind was already scampering ahead.

"So, this is the posse come to arrest me, is it?"

Said in the right way, this could have been an acceptable little joke. But Franklin sneered as he spoke, and the contempt in his eyes was palpable.

Brendan had a response. "Well. I forgot to put on my sheriff's star, Frank, so this arrest may be invalid. Anyway, I was thinking of buying a new three-piece suite, and I heard you were getting rid of some furniture."

This cool and easy remark took Franklin aback and wrong-footed him. It was then that he noticed the goat. With big, curly horns and a little straggly beard, it gazed steadily at him with its golden eyes, standing quietly between Ruth and Betsy. That was what startled him the most; the goat was not on all fours but standing on its hind hooves.

"Why'd you bring that? What the hell? Who brought that goat?"

He pointed at it and they looked.

Brendan said, "There's nothing there. Did you say, 'a goat'?"

Betsy looked around and spoke to the frozen Franklin. "Maybe it was just this you saw."

She pointed to a piece of stained-glass window which shone rather golden in the light behind them. It had some shapes worked in that might have been mistaken for animals, or perhaps, angels.

Franklin was not fooled. But this was no time to explain. It had gone. Between the women, a two-feet space, a lit window behind. He took a deep breath and recovered some control.

"Yes, well, I know it's been on the grapevine that I'm moving out, but, I'm still considering my options. We should all do that, doncha think, Betsy? Consider your options?"

Betsy was not yet ready to participate in this tense set-to.

Ruth observed. "Frankie's got some new, saucy girlfriends – did you know? Bebette and – did I hear right – Lucille? Oo-la-la."

"They're not girlfriends. I tried to tell you. But as usual, your mind was closed."

"Well, Frankie, you can blame many things on my closed mind, but not this. Ok, so they're not girlfriends. I'm prepared to believe that, because I do not see any woman willingly being your girlfriend; never mind two at once. So, what's the story?"

Frankie saw he was cornered. Always game to take on anybody in single combat, he failed to recall anything that would convince these three, quite different, people. He cursed himself for not getting a story prepared for this encounter. And so, against every grain of his person, he thought he would try, for once, telling the truth.

"Youse better sit down," he said. "This could take a long time."

Betsy stood. The others sat.

"There's a group – a company of men –all in Glasgow or round about, who got an idea to start up an organisation that would meet certain needs they all had. No, don't jump to conclusions, please. Let me explain. Two of these old guys – they're all over seventy, maybe over eighty – have been friends all their life; knew one another, knew their likes and tastes and had shared many experiences through life. Their lives had branched apart for about fifteen years and then reunited, both as widowers. Once, joking about sex, they started to talk seriously about—"

Betsy interrupted. "Sorry, Frankie, but I know you more than some people do. And I can tell when I—"

"Whoa, whoa! Can I ask you for a minute to think about 'The Full Monty' and change it to 'The Full Monica'?"

"I don't want to hear any more. You're pimping women for some dirty, old, impotent men. Of course, you won't say it like that. You'll dress it up in frills. You're good at that, Frankie. I've watched you deceive people. You're a master-deceiver. But not us. Not this time."

"You didn't let me get started," protested Frankie. "Give me a chance."

Ruth re-entered the fray. "Franklin, just forget all this stuff about old men drooling over Bebette. Just stick to this. What job or role do you have in Anniesland College? And if you admit that you don't work there, then where is your income coming from? Because you sure aren't short of money. What's the source? And don't invent any blethers about investments."

"Hey, if I want to discuss my personal finances, I won't feel I should invite your family over for the discussion. We came to a good arrangement about income – it was one you were happy with. You have no financial insecurity here. But you can't put me on trial like this. What are the charges, for a start?"

"Listen, for once in your life, Franklin. It's over with us. I can get somewhere else, but it'll take a couple of weeks. I'd like you to stay somewhere else for that time, and as soon as I'm gone, you can move back in. Can you do that for me?"

Franklin's bags were packed, and he was set to leave there and then, but he took a chance to hesitate; to pretend to think it over as if it was a huge demand on him. This went on for a bit, and then he agreed he would do that.

"I need a coupla days," he lied. "Betsy can put you up until then. Can you do that, Betsy?"

"For a couple of days. Do not wriggle out of this, Franklin. Or it'll be war."

"Oh, listen to that! Brendan, your wife's a warrior now."

Brendan looked silently at Franklin for ten seconds, then replied, "Frankie, can we cut all this stuff out? All this masquerade? Let's leave aside all this stuff we've been talking about. I have an idea. An offer. I don't know what you work at, or if you work at all, but you could come and work with me. It won't make you rich, but it'll give you a regular routine. It'll keep you on an even keel, and it'll give you a new interest to get your mind into. And it's healthy, outdoor work. I believe it would do you a lot of good. This is not the girls' idea – they just want rid of you. I'm offering you something more. I don't like using a cliché like 'it's a fresh start', but it is that sort of thing."

The tightness faded from Franklin's face, and he passed a flickering smile round the three of them. He sensed Betsy was about to intervene and object, so he said,

"That's very brotherly of you, Brendan. Very kind. Of course, I know little of your line of work with trees and all that. But I can see the attractions in the picture you present. I'm interested, Brendan. However—"

Betsy cut in. "There's always a 'however' with you."

Franklin paused and smiled sweetly at Betsy. "However, I cannot give you an immediate answer. There are certain things afoot that I must sort out. I am very hopeful they'll be sorted out by tomorrow evening. But until I get this situation fixed, I just couldn't say yes to anything. Soon as I know where I stand, I'll ring you, Brendan."

It was a bravura little cameo, and Franklin thought he had the three of them totally puzzled. He had sounded grateful and appreciative but had covered his tracks skilfully. He stood up and tried to think of a remark that would bring this episode to an end.

"Look, Ruth, please feel free to stay here from tomorrow night. I'll be out of your way then. And contact me, however you like, when you know that you'll be gone for good."

Betsy added. "You're a very cold, cold person, Franklin. Ice cold. And, you're seeing goats? I would get to a doctor soon if I was you."

"Thank you, Betsy. Your concern for my health has always been one of the things I admired in you."

Chapter 7

"Dad, do you get paid a lot for driving a bus?"

"No. Not a lot. Enough to make sure that on a Friday night you get plenty of fish and chips."

"You're so common, Johnny," said his mother. "Can't you give the boy something higher to aim for than fish and chips? You have no ambition, but Franklin does. You should be feeding those ambitions, not just feeding his stomach."

"Mum, I like fish and chips. But Dad, say if you drove the bus for six days instead of five, would you get more money?"

"I would, but I need my rest days like everybody else."

"How much extra would you get for working on a Saturday?"

"What is all this, Franklin? This is becoming an interrogation. Carmella, do you encourage this prying into my wages? How about you, too, give the boy something higher to think about and aim for?"

"No, Dad, it's not that. But if you brought in a little extra, maybe we could also have pudding on a Friday. Or a Sunday. On Tuesday, Delia showed me a new

DVD player she got from her dad. She said it was because he had got a bonus that week. Do you ever get bonuses, Dad? What is a bonus, anyway?"

"Who's Delia?" asked his mother.

"My girlfriend. Well, maybe. Dad, can you get bonuses? Maybe if you worked on a Sunday."

"Hey, this boy won't give up, Carmella. And now he has a girlfriend. Haul him off, please."

Franklin and his father mock-wrestled, but only briefly, not to let the chips get cold.

Johnny's life, like many bus drivers, ran on a cycle of shifts, and often these did not coincide with regular family hours, so for Franklin, getting a few hours with his dad was a luxury, especially on a Friday night when his dad was always relaxed and friendly. His mother got her pay, so she was in a good mood, and he got his pocket money, which he had been glad to notice had been increasing recently without any explanation. Maybe Dad was getting bonuses after all, and not mentioning it aloud.

Then one day, he overheard his parents in conversation, which Franklin noticed was more hushed than usual. He liked secrets. He crept closer and listened. But all he could make out was that his dad, from the following week, would be on a split shift, and that this was good because it gave him more time for the other work, and that Carmella would have to be very careful about who she spoke to about this work. Franklin considered what this 'other work' might be.

Probably not a spy or a detective; maybe part of a neighbourhood watch group – he had been hearing about them. Maybe even something bad, like housebreaking or kidnapping, though he dismissed that thought as ridiculous. Many possibilities presented themselves to him. He decided to keep listening for more information.

Often, when the three of them were together, the talk would be loud and boisterous as ever. But on occasion, if the parents thought Frankie was occupied with the TV or some distraction, they would speak more softly. Franklin would be listening, and slowly pieced together part of the picture of the forthcoming new work. He felt excited and a little scared.

It would involve night work. It would involve more than just his dad, perhaps several others. It seemed to make his dad jumpier and more nervous than his mother, although he had not picked up any signs that she was involved in this project. She had always seemed to him to be cool and fearless in all situations, and he really loved this in her. It placed her above any of his friends' mothers.

One night at, eleven o'clock, he was reading by torchlight under the bedcovers. He heard his dad come downstairs slowly, as if he was carrying something, then some muffled sounds, and then his dad opened the front door, put the snib on the lock and went out. In a flash, Franklin was out of bed, into his hooded jacket, holding onto his reading torch, and silently slipped out after his father. Dad was a hundred yards away, but Franklin soon brought that down to thirty yards, staying in the shadows. His father was carrying some bulky box or case which, lucky for Franklin, was awkward and slowed him down. Johnny turned north onto London Road and was joined by another figure, wrapped, tall and long-striding. Franklin suddenly felt fear; felt how dangerous all this might be, and he hesitated. The tall figure now took over carrying the box, and they picked up speed, and Franklin began to fall behind. He stopped and gave up – angry at his weakness – and turned for home.

Back in bed, as he turned out the light, he saw that it had all happened in less than half an hour. He fell asleep immediately.

Over the next months, Johnny made several night trips. Sometimes Franklin was awake, but he never again followed his father. One Sunday, his father had left the garden hut unlocked, and Franklin naturally peered in to see if there was anything interesting. At the back, in the dark, he saw the strangely shaped box his father had been carrying that night. He examined it but didn't dare touch it. It had two silver locks and a very sturdy handle. Its shape still puzzled and scared him. It was so strange, in the same way that some coffins are. But it was too small to be a coffin.

Then, on the first Friday in May, Franklin came home from school to find his father already home, having been on an early shift. There was a present for

Franklin – his dad said he could call it a bonus. It was a telescope. Franklin had a great interest in astronomy, and he bounced for joy and started right away into reading the booklet that told how to use the telescope. The nearest, true dark sky to Glasgow was far south, in Galloway Forest, but the part of the city where the Gaddarinis lived had remarkably few lights. And it included the wide darkness of St Michael's Cemetery. So Franklin got very excited. Only then did he notice that his mother was wearing a stunning, beautiful, green dress.

"Mum! That is sensational Is that a bonus too?"

"Bonuses all round this weekend," said Johnny.

Carmella said she was going for the fish and chips, but not in her new dress – it was far too classy for the Chippy.

Peering back through the swirls of his memory, Franklin thought it might have been about this time that things changed. He was aware, at secondary school, that he was not as tough as many boys were. Perhaps that was in his mind one lunchtime, as he trotted home from school, cutting through side streets and lanes. Then, all in one blurred movement, he slowed slightly, picked up a sizeable stone from the pavement and hurled it through the window of a ground-floor flat in Farthing Street. The thrill he got made him soar. He was flying on wings of fear and delight, regret and exhilaration, and he had to stop and breathe deeply to recover. He did not use that route for many weeks afterwards. He thought often about what might have happened; maybe an old lady had been sitting near the window, and got badly cut, or a little child was scarred. The thoughts were too much for him. He told no one. The memory never left him.

Just as strange was the occasion, during this period, when he broke into the house of his school pal, Donald Deigan. Franklin's memory was less sharp on the details of this event. For example, it was a weekday afternoon, so why was he not at school? The Deigans were a big family who lived in a tenement ground-floor flat in Penn Street. Franklin, sauntering along, noticed that their living room window was lowered by about six inches. He strolled over, nipped up onto the window ledge and easily used the sash to pull the window fully down. Then he climbed in. How reckless. There were many Deigans in the family, and there was a strong chance that one of them would be at home. But no – the house was empty. Franklin took a slow look through it. There was nothing to take. There was no sign, whatsoever, of riches. There was hardly any sign of life. They were poor people. There were some coins on the mantelpiece, but not worth bothering with. After a bit, he climbed out, raised the window back up and skipped away. A neighbour opposite had seen him come and go and reported the incident to Mrs Deigan.

The next day, Donald challenged Franklin on the subject, but he did so privately, and Franklin expressed great sorrow and said he hadn't a clue what he was thinking and swore he had not taken a single item. Weirdly, it was never spoken of again and was another incident to take its immortal place in the gallery of Franklin's mind.

The third in this line of memorable sins or crimes was the one which brought this period in Franklin's life to a head. Two streets along from Franklin, lived his cousin, Giorgio, also a Gaddarini. He was a year older than Franklin and already carving a rather fearsome reputation. Franklin liked to think of Giorgio, in the school year ahead of him, as his protector. They often met up and walked to school together – on the days, that is, that Giorgio was not too busy to go to school.

One day, Giorgio opened one hand to show Franklin what he was holding. It was a little bundle of pound notes. Giorgio peeled three off his stash and handed them to Franklin.

"Buy yerself something. But try and keep it quiet. Don't go blabbin'."

Speechless and amazed, Franklin nodded and didn't dare ask for any explanation.

"We're cousins – remember that. We are Gaddarinis."

He took Franklin in a mock neck lock and whispered in a kind of Italian, "Now we are blood brothers. *Capisce?* I die for you. You die for me." He added, "Always keep it a secret."

On the way back from school, Franklin took several longcuts to be able to think what he was to do and how he was to hide the money from his parents. But he found out right away that he was very adept at this and found deception quite straightforward – he had the face for it.

He got a further payment from Giorgio the next week. By then, he had bought a couple of toy cars, some football magazines and a lot of ice cream, and he had also bought Donald Deigan a full bottle of Irn-Bru and a pudding supper. He also paid for a toy car for Donald.

Here came the fatal flaw. Donald's father got suspicious and paid a visit to the Gaddarinis. Only then did it all come out. Cousin Giorgio, in addition to his parents and two brothers, had a sick great-uncle living with them, mostly bed-ridden. Giorgio had sussed that this uncle, Bill, kept his money in a wallet at the edge of his bed. Giorgio would wait until the uncle had to go to the toilet and would pounce and make off with a few pounds at a time. The uncle, being nearly blind, made it easy in the short-term, but of course, the scam was doomed.

Johnny talked long to his son, enough to bring Franklin real feelings of shame and disappointment. He handed over the little money he still had left. Johnny added the balance and paid the money back to his brother. Marco, Giorgio's dad, was less forgiving and hammered Giorgio so mercilessly, that he didn't appear at school for two weeks.

All he said to Franklin was, "It was great while it lasted. Especially the beer." Giorgio was 12.

These episodes, which Franklin never forgot, settled deep in some vault inside him, and he withdrew them many times to use as a beacon or guide when the matter of doing wrong appeared in his life. What was good, and why should anyone do good, were questions he thought about, even when at primary school. Twice he had escaped being caught, and on another occasion, he had got off with a lecture. Was his father's kindness misplaced? When he saw Giorgio's black eye and how he now limped, he fretted over being let off. If he had got beaten, it might well have acted as a deterrent, for he was afraid of pain. And it might have given him some status and solidarity with his punished cousin.

He had become an altar server in his parish church, Sacred Heart, and in so doing had made the company of some different lads, mostly less dangerous than his previous gang. He got to like serving at Mass and Benediction and got to learn the names for all the paraphernalia around the altar.

After three years, when he was at secondary school, his behaviour had levelled out, and there had been no further events that left him sick with fear and confusion. His father was pleased that he had kept on with the altar-serving and encouraged it. Less so his mother. Once, Franklin overheard them talking about the church and the services.

His mother said, "Yes, a black soutane – that would be all right. But those red soutanes, along with those frilly surplices and that ridiculous medallion on a red rope, makes them look like a bunch of little pansies."

Franklin felt the rage rise in his chest. He also felt strong resentment that his attempts to take part in something good and worthwhile were being mocked – and by his mother! There was a taste of bile in his mouth, and he never again thought of his mother in the same way.

Only the week before, he had come back home early from the boxing club, gone through the back door and heard voices. It was his mother talking to a man called Patrick.

Franklin had seen Patrick looking at his mother on Sundays after Mass; examining her closely when he thought no one was watching him, in a way that made Franklin shiver a little.

He sneaked a look. They were sitting across from one another, and there was a bottle of wine on the low table between them. His dad was at work. Franklin waited and heard a little of their conversation.

Patrick said, "It's a fine book. I know you'll enjoy it. I just knew you would have high taste in the arts. Do you know, I've had the privilege of seeing the originals of some of these paintings, where they hang in galleries or on Church walls throughout the world. But especially Italy, of course – your own country."

"Where I lived in Verona, there was art everywhere. We just took it for granted – a gallery was a gallery; a bar was a bar. When I was growing up there, I had other interests on my mind."

"Did you ever visit the other great cities? Rome? Venice?"

"I never went there, no."

"Did you ever go back to Italy?"

"No."

"Would you like to?"

Franklin was aware of a long pause at this point, and when his mother glanced in his direction, he knew it was time to back out of there. He felt rather sick in his stomach, and he could not explain why.

Chapter 8

Franklin had recalled these events, and others like them, many times over his life, though rarely did they crowd in on him as forcefully as they had just done. He checked the time and saw that he had been sitting on the sofa for nearly two hours, in a kind of reverie. He tried now to bring himself into the present and to sort out his thoughts and feelings for what lay ahead, not from the distant past.

The effect of the earlier alcohol was thinning, and he had his first doubts about the proposed journey to Ireland. What was he thinking? How was it going to help him? What did he hope to find there except more booze, more cronies and more lies? He stood and gave himself a physical shake or two, did some stretches, paced around, then sat down again and spoke to himself in a low tone.

The best part of this idea was when I told myself that nobody would know where I had gone. That was what thrilled me the most. But, did I need the secrecy? I could've told several people – Ruth, Buster, Dave, even Jem – and not one of them would've cared or tried to stop me. In fact, I have a feeling every one of them would be more than glad to see me go. They would have said, 'Have a good long break', 'Don't hurry back', 'About time, you could use a real break'. All lies – payback for the hundreds of lies I've told to them. Must have been some time, long ago, I suppose, when I made the decision that love would not be my goal; would not even be in my plans. What was it, anyway? Brought nothing but trouble. I suppose I still think that. Just look at the state I'm in right here and now. Hoping, as usual, that making a change is the answer. Any change will do. Jump in a car and drive far away, and when you come back, the air will be pure and clear of dust. You'll be able to breath once again. So here we are, on the one road...

He started singing an old song. "We're on the one road// It may be a long road// But we're together now, who cares?"

But that, too, was a lie. Franklin was not together with anybody.

He put down his depressed mood to alcohol withdrawal but decided to drink no more that evening, having to drive down to Stranraer, then a couple of hours on the ferry across to Larne, then a further long drive to Dublin.

His mind kept taking him away back to his childhood. To get a break from this, and because he had not been dreaming much recently, he took his three priadel tablets and he went to bed. Sleep did not come for many hours. But when the alarm clock rang at seven, he was alert. And as soon as he came awake, he knew he had changed his mind yet again.

He had fixed on what was really bothering him – the meeting with Mr Patrick – and knew for certain that if he missed that meeting, he would spend the whole time in Ireland nervous, agitated and fearful. This issue had to be faced squarely. It could not be avoided. At eight thirty, he called the Stena Line again, cancelled his booking, and rebooked for two p.m. the following day. He called his cousin, Tommy, and said he was sorry – it would be the next day for his visit. Tommy was known to one and all as a tolerant man. Immediately, Franklin felt his spirits lift, and his mind felt sharper to prepare for the meeting at *The Resting Place*.

Almost ready to leave, he took a check in the mirror and was not satisfied with the casual image he saw. He changed into a more formal suit, shirt and tie. Just as he was about to turn the ignition in his car, he had another change of plan. He got his packed suitcase out of the boot, carried it up to his flat and left it there. He had a feeling, that was all.

At one forty-five, he was strolling among the tombs of The Levels, as Mr Patrick had counselled. He looked at the headstone of a Molly Malone – surely some girl named in honour of the heroine of Irish song, rather than the original Molly. Yet, strangely, beneath the words 'alive, alive-o', the dates were born 18 --, died 19 --. Then he took a five-minute stroll among the lower gravestones. He made a turn he hadn't noticed before, through a laburnum archway and along a soft and leafy path between deep green shrubbery, in which the gravestones had been sunk well back. When he emerged from this cloister, there was a stretch of unused lawn which he strolled across to see what lay beyond. He pulled up sharp on the unexpected verge of a very steep slope that plunged for about one hundred metres. Down at the bottom was a pond or small lake, or maybe an old quarry which had been allowed to fill. He could see ripples on the surface, and there seemed to be a current in it, but he was too far to be sure. He was also suffering from vertigo, as there was no wall or fence at the bottom, but only some large kerbstones where the hill met the water, such as are sometimes placed around reservoirs.

Just out of his vision to the left, he sensed some animals were grazing. They looked like pigs. Franklin paused and stretched his neck to see over the ridge. No, he decided, they must be sheep. He found his way back through the archway to familiar territory and checked his watch.

Careful to be most punctual, he drove around the hill and in to *The Resting Place* carpark. To his surprise, there were a lot of cars already parked – he counted ten. Tam came out to greet him, more deferential than pleasant, a serious expression replacing the previous affability. He led Franklin upstairs, then downstairs, then into a waiting area. Tam pointed to an easy chair and withdrew.

Two thirty. *Good. Deep breaths; that's it. Plead carelessness and plead distraction – no more. No jokes. Whatever else, no jokes. God, what a house this is. You wouldn't know it from outside. It's massive. Look at that ceiling. I think, right here, we're underground.*

A door opened, and a woman came through and walked straight up to Franklin.

"Franklin! It's you! You'll be all right – they're in a good mood. They're a lovely old crew. Well, except for that cranky James. He's a nasty bastard. Big spider. Just don't say too much. You'll be all right. That little bitch Bebette – no gratitude, no loyalty. And speaking on my behalf! My sainted arse, she will! They're running a little ahead of time, so it'll be you soon. Good luck."

"Wait! Lucille, Lucille, I hardly recognised you. You look great. I've been trying to plan what to say, but now I don't know. You think they won't take Bebette's side? It would be useful for me to know."

"I can see that. But I don't know, either. They don't give much away. Must rush. Whatever happens, nice knowing you, Franklin."

"Which one is James?"

But she was gone. No sooner had one door closed behind Lucille, than the door at the far end opened, and a man of about Tam's age and apparel looked down towards Franklin and beckoned for him to approach.

The room he entered was nothing like the comfy lounge of a few days ago. This was dark and heavily curtained, with no chink of daylight, and a long business table in the centre. At the top of the table, two people sat, with four others down each side and a place for Franklin to sit at the bottom end. He took a glance round and firstly was surprised to see that two of the ten were women; one immediately to his right and the other at the top of the table. The second surprise was to see a laptop computer at each place, including his. His anxiety shot up. Did they have recordings of his sins and crimes?

The chairman at the top spoke. "Good afternoon, Mr Gaddarini. My name is Kurt, and this lady is Veronica. The others you will pick up as we go along.

"This is our Spring meeting, and we found some space in it to deal with a behavioural matter that might be damaging to our group. We started today at eleven. We got some good business dealt with, and now lastly, we come to you, Mr Gaddarini. I will put you at ease right away. We are not dealing with offences of the highest order. The outcome of our deliberations should still leave you continuing as one of us. However, all faults and flaws in systems must be properly attended to and repaired, or they will return and threaten the whole system. And we may have to agree to some measures of adjustment."

He paused and sat back, and Franklin took the chance to see Mr Patrick, down beside Veronica, and Mr Mick, second on his left. He also recognised George, second on his right. He did not yet know the name of the beautiful woman sitting immediately on his right.

Veronica stood up. "Mr Gaddarini. We'll make it Franklin if that is agreeable to you. It's not a court, after all, and you're not on trial. In fact, you're acquainted with several of the gentlemen here. This is just a slightly different context. We're all fond of games and rituals and rules, and so on. Now, you have been with the group for three years and two months, as a C member. Your record is not without blemish, but you have no serious incidents recorded against you. Apart from a few early slips in protocol, you have earned your rewards. Over the last few months, your reliability has been a little less convincing, your earlier consistency has been less evident. And maybe it is within that context that your current difficulties lie."

She started to pour herself a glass of water and lifted some papers and scanned them. Meantime, Franklin checked out the company. He could easily imagine these ten people sitting rather hunched over, wearing the hoods of the Inquisition judges. It was starting to scare him, despite Kurt's opening assurances.

"Franklin, my task now is to set out simply the nature of the code violations as we see them. You will then be invited to discuss these and offer any explanations you think relevant. On Sunday 21st, you were the cause of an act of public disorder which drew much attention throwing an armchair straight out through a window and down into the street; public disorder that drew adverse attention to yourself. Secondly, this same incident led to a police interrogation which, again, threatened bad publicity. And thirdly, the wildly erratic nature of the incident must raise questions as to your required stability of character. These are three aspects of the one situation. And there is a second situation that is much more directly a concern to us in this group. Despite the known injunction of the society that no business is to be conducted at the member's own home, you engaged in business discussion with a B member, number seventy-one, in your own home, yesterday morning. This lapse was compounded by the fact that the discussion was overheard by your own partner, who is, of course, not a member, and in doing so you were the cause of member seventy-one leaving the society. Thirdly, member seventy-one tried to persuade B member seventy-eight also to leave. Member seventy-eight is, at present, thinking over what she should do.

"We will pause for a few minutes to allow you time to gather your thoughts and present a response to the concerns I have just raised on behalf of the society."

Franklin made an effort to focus but was interrupted by a touch on his sleeve from the woman on his right. She was a very good-looking woman about his own age.

She smiled and said, "You're looking worried. Don't be. I know how this works. I'm Marilyn, by the way. You'll be given something to do to show you're sorry. We're a bunch of old teddy bears, really. Just relax. Don't say too much. Oh, in case you're not aware, you should address Kurt as 'Brother' and Veronica –and me – as 'Sister'.

Invited to speak, Franklin stood and shivered. Someone had said it wasn't a court. Maybe it was a weird sort of cabaret –all those distinguished faces down there looking up at The Phantom of the Opera.

"The first incident – the chair – was no one's fault but mine. I thank God that nobody got hurt. I had a lit taper, lighting some candles, and a spark jumped onto the chair without me seeing. After a minute somebody shouted, 'Look!' And there was a flame coming from the chair. What happened next, I do not remember, except having one purpose – to get rid of the danger of fire. Where I got the strength from, the Lord only knows. Maybe I was momentarily given super strength to deal with a heroic problem. Excuse me, I feel a bit dizzy."

Franklin was sweating badly. He drank some water and took a deep breath. "Anyway, as I say, nobody got injured. I got a glazier in right away, and he did a right good job of replacing the window and casement. I paid him a good bit extra – he deserved it. I went for a drink to calm my nerves. Later, we had to speak to the police, and they accepted my account. The matter is closed. For the bad publicity it attracted to the society, I am deeply sorry."

He paused and looked around, wondering if he should continue or wait for any questions. Everyone continued to look at him. He felt his eyes go in and out of focus, and he supported himself with his hands on the table.

"As to the second matter, I am more at fault, because I have been told exactly what the rules are, and I thought, having been operating quite well for a couple of years, that I was rule-proof. And I just got careless. The place for our assignment was close by. I thought my partner would by that hour be at work, so I suggested we use my house. She did not object. I did not know my partner, suffering from a hangover from a night out, was still in her room and overheard the conversation between me and Bebette – that is, member B seventy-one.

"The member, totally surprised by the presence of somebody unexpected, panicked a little. She was suspicious of the whole meeting, told me she was withdrawing her services and left. She added that member B seventy-eight would also withdraw when she heard about this event. I applied no pressure or force of any kind during this incident. The harm that was done was in the loss of one or two B members. This arose from unfounded suspicion. But the suspicion came from my failure to keep to the laid-down instructions. I am to blame. I am truly sorry. If there is a way in which I can make amends, I am ready to hear it."

Franklin sat down.

Brother Kurt announced that anyone who had any questions or observations should indicate their wish by raising their right hand. Franklin, beginning to wonder where he was, noticed, again, the height of the ceiling and wondered how deep underground this room was. It was a committee room in the traditional style – dark wood panelled walls; low discreet lighting; the air ancient with thoughts. *We might be beside or below the cemetery here,* he reflected.

A hand was raised. "Mr Gaddarini, I'm Brother James. About the fire in the chair. I have to say it does not have the ring of truth. The spark sent from a taper you use to light a candle is a very weak thing and would not have caused any fire. A flame that you say did appear could easily have been smothered and extinguished quickly. I see no need for your decision to lift the chair and throw it out. And I should add that the power and dexterity needed to lift an armchair and hurl it through a window are quite extraordinary. And yet, in your record, there are no previous signs whatsoever of you having such extraordinary strength. This must be noted here as a strange and unnatural ability. The outcome is perhaps immaterial, but your state of mind preceding the incident gives me cause for concern. It suggests a manic unpredictability. This is a trait we strive to avoid in all our members."

Franklin turned pale and looked astonished. While wracking his brains, Brother Kurt called to him that no reply was expected.

Another hand was raised. "Brother Bart. Mr Gaddarini, at the core of our society is a belief in the purity and balanced tension between sensuality and innocence. Our B members arrive and, in due course, leave, and will leave for reasons of health or age or changing circumstances. But never, ever through mistreatment from A members or C members. Perhaps the incident with Bebette did not amount to mistreatment, but it fell short of the standards we require. I am not convinced that you grasp this. I mean, can your mind operate at this level – a spiritual and aesthetic level – above the commercial and administrative levels which also tie in to our society? If it cannot, you must tell us, honestly and directly, before you leave the meeting today."

Franklin had time to look more carefully at Brother Bart who was seated down beside Patrick at the far end. Wild of hair and beard, he fulfilled the role of the lunatic that a film director might want to have in a film of such a meeting. But his words were far from insane, and Franklin had enjoyed listening to his strange, poetic voice, glad that he was not required to respond, because his mind did not usually feed on concepts such as those presented by Brother Bart.

Sister Marilyn raised her hand. "Mr Gaddarini, are you planning on leaving home for a while? A short break, perhaps, or a holiday? I would like you to answer."

Franklin was dumbfounded. How could anyone know of his plans for heading to Ireland? How could anyone know when he hardly knew himself? The only safe route here was to play dumb.

", I have been under a bit of strain recently. My partner and I are running through a period of problems – difficulties. Maybe, as little as a break would be suitable, yes, it has been crossing my mind."

"Nothing definitely fixed yet, though?"

"No. Not yet."

He caught the eye of Marilyn and saw she had a little smile on her lips, and she had a look in her eye that showed she did not believe him. He gulped and tried to smile but failed.

Another hand was raised. "Brother Patrick. Mr Gaddarini, trust of one another is of the highest value in this little society. What we as a body want to know above all is that you can be trusted, unconditionally. If we can trust you, then we can move ahead. But just before that, I do have a question. Did you remember to deal with that little request I made of you the other day?"

Franklin's mind was blank. Wrapped up in this piece of gothic theatre, he had trouble thinking back to anything before the present.

He shook his head. "Sorry, it must have slipped my mind. I... I just don't remember your request."

"Oh, don't worry, Mr Gaddarini. It's not urgent. But I did ask you to bring me a photograph of your mother."

"Of course you did. And I will. But please understand, I've had my hands full with these problems we're discussing. It's only been a couple of days. I will bring you one, I promise."

After a short, unbroken silence, Brother Kurt stood up. "I thank the members for their attendance and their participation. There is one further item on the agenda for A members. Meantime, Mr Gaddarini, you will, within a few days, receive a secure email providing details of our decisions in these matters. The message may also contain an invitation for you to carry out some piece of work. It is important that you do not delay in responding to that invitation. Thank you, Mr Gaddarini. C member Zia will show you the way out."

A small, oriental woman appeared out of nowhere from behind where Franklin was sitting and asked him to come with her. A few upstairs, downstairs, turns and corridors later, he was in the front hallway, and Zia, unsmiling, was opening the front door for him.

Back in the boardroom, quiet conversations were going on in low voices. Kurt called the members to refocus and reminded them of their right to suggest paths of action following a serious breach of the club's rules. One member reminded his fellows that they mustn't overreact. All breaches were serious, but in this case, only slight damage had been done, and only slight danger might accrue. This view was challenged by James, who saw weakness and threat in a soft reaction. Patrick could see that James wanted Franklin got rid of – from membership, that is – but pointed out the same old difficulty here: how could they guarantee security and silence if a C member left under bad terms? Marilyn said that the two B members had not actually left yet and might be persuaded to stay if removed from the influence of Mr Gaddarini.

In the end, it was agreed that Franklin must be censured, and penalised financially, and set a task, by Mr Kurt, to re-establish his good faith and commitment.

PART TWO

Chapter 9

Franklin had never known the fresh air of outdoors to be so embracing. He did not get into his car right away and felt he would enjoy a little stroll. Though far from elated, he felt he had done well and had got off lightly, and he was soon able to attribute this to his own powers of escaping from danger, whatever it might be. Gaddarini wins again! One part of his brain was having this silly, childish party and celebration, but another was noticing the cars that sat round Franklin's Nissan. He recognised a Bentley, a Volvo, a modest Ford, a long sedan with shaded windows, but also one car with no badge or name or insignia to identify it – solid black in all dimensions. And near it was another car with no number plates, neither front nor back. However, he'd had enough mystery for one day, and the celebration side won easily. Off he went to the *Ewe and Lamb*, hoping there would be regulars whom he could enthral with his latest adventures.

Then he reconsidered. He had been given mercy; he had been offered a chance to show he had high standards. Blabbing about his exploits in a pub was suddenly abhorrent to him. He remembered he had a busy day coming up and decided to make for home.

At home, he suddenly felt tired and took a nap. At eight thirty, he was in his usual place in the *Ewe and Lamb*. Old Friends, Terry and Batty, were over on a visit and were glad to see him. Lizzie and Duke joined them around nine, and then at nine thirty, the Arab arrived. His appearance displayed boldly that he was a native of the great desert.

He cruised over and resumed on a theme he had lately been pestering Franklin with. "So, Franklin, you have still not taken that pretty wife of yours on a little holiday. It's a shame. You must see she needs a holiday. In the sun somewhere. That's why I'm always telling you, I can arrange that."

"Haven't I heard this before, Mustafa? You seem to think I can't organise a holiday for myself."

"For yourself – yes, but not for Ruth. She needs a break, Frank. There are some wonderful places in Iraq I could take her – I mean, arrange a visit for her."

"You think I'd send any woman alone to Iraq for a holiday? Come on. What about Cyprus or Rhodes?"

"No, no, I have no connections there. But listen – the place I'm really thinking of is Babylon."

"What? You just said Iraq."

"Babylon is just beside it; a mystical place – many songs written about Babylon. But she should bring somebody with her – a girlfriend, maybe."

"Or a sister?" asked Franklin, the words spoken before he had even formed the idea. "How would that do?"

"A sister? She has a sister. Ideal! Yes."

"And you think I can sell this holiday to these two women?"

"No, no, Frank. I do the selling. I explain everything. When I have finished, they will be running for the aeroplane! All you need to do is to introduce me to these two fine ladies. I met Ruth once. I'm sure her sister will be as charming."

"Yes, no doubt. I'll let you find out for yourself about that one."

"So we have a deal? I say deal because this is more complicated than I have been saying. Business interests in Baghdad are desperate to have Western presence in the cities. Especially to have Western women being seen in the streets and shops and squares. It will work miracles for business and progress and, someday, freedom in my country. For this reason, women from the UK are safe. In no danger. Iraqis and Babylonians are fascinated to see westerners moving happily around their great city. It is a great sign of hope."

"That's all very well, Mustafa, but at this very moment, my beloved and I are not on the best of terms."

"You have a quarrel? A lover's argument? No problem – happens all the time. And what better way to heal a wound than to bring her an offer of a lovely holiday for her and her sister. You need to tell me a little more about the girls; their background and so on…"

"How come? Why is that needed?"

"Just so I can have a pleasant conversation, knowing a little about their history; nothing more. And, of course, to get back to that deal I mentioned earlier, some of the businessmen I mentioned will show their gratitude for initiatives like this, and you and I will benefit, Frank, I can assure you. Possibly in a lovely little town near Baghdad, called Basra. You have heard of it?"

"Yeah. Near the sea, isn't it? Ruth would insist that any holiday is right by the sea."

"Oh, yes. Very near. A short walk. One of the best beaches in the Middle East."

"Right. I'm getting good vibes about this, Mustafa."

This was not true. Franklin couldn't get excited about this, benefits or not. He was more focused on getting Betsy out of his hair and maybe into a more friendly disposition towards him, and maybe this was the way. And Ruth was already on the way out of his hair.

A vague memory from childhood came to him of reading *Tales of the Arabian Nights*, a book he remembered fondly. The image startled him, then faded.

By now, Franklin was nearly drunk and was trying to keep in mind that he had an early start next morning. But the jokes and the banter were rising, and inevitably there came a call for a song. Franklin was right off the blocks with a rousing version of *The Rising of the Moon*, a close imitation of the Tommy Makem version of that ballad. Rapturous applause was followed by Duke's interpretation of Leonard Cohen's *Bird on a Wire*, which turned the mood agreeably maudlin, leaving Batty to hit rock bottom with the evergreen *I'm Nobody's Child*.

The Arab leaned over to Franklin. "Not place for business matters, Frank. You got my number. Call me in the morning. You're the man."

A couple of classic pub songs later, and Franklin was in paradise, vaguely aware that today had been victorious and happy and that tomorrow was to be looked forward to with confidence.

Sitting out on one of the upper decks on the good ship, *Juliana*, Franklin tried to relax. Here he was, like a little kid going on his summer holiday. The weather was breezy but fair. A few passengers were strolling around or leaning on the rails, and several of them looked at Franklin and smiled. When a man of his own age smiled and nodded his head towards him, Franklin realised he himself had had a smile on his face for ten minutes. His smile was creating further smiles. *How odd,* he thought. *Maybe I don't smile enough. I must work and practice on my smiling. Bound to be beneficial. People are obviously pleased to see my face with a smile on it.*

They're thinking, 'What a nice friendly man'. What do they know?

They smiled back at the smiling man. Franklin quickly tired of this insanity and reset the muscles in his face.

He had made the run to Larne in good time, and only now did he start to think about what he was going to do in Ireland. He presumed that most of the time he would spend in Dublin, being a city boy through and through. At that moment, he had no plan for touring – even though with the car it would have been easy – Limerick, Galway and the West, Killarney and the Lakes. He had seen them all more than once, but in Dublin, and especially its North side, he had always felt at home. Tommy, his host, would be sure to introduce him to shoals of acquaintances, as usual, and there would be lots of proposals from among them about the things he must do and must see while he was there. Not long after he left the port of Larne, he stopped in to top up the petrol and then was on his way.

Taking a short stop in Dundalk, he found that an old favourite, *Gulliver's Café*, had been taken over, so he had a good meal in *The Jockey's Bar* – steak and onions, with a jacket potato, that could only be Irish. Then on to Dublin and arrival at *The Five Lamps* on North Strand Road. A quick turn down Amiens Street, and he was knocking on the door of Tommy Jordan.

"There ye are now, Frankie. Let's have a look at ya. Mm… not too good. Tired; worried maybe. I have the gift, d'ye see – I can sense a person's mood by an early look over his face. And the lines I see on your face are not running in the right direction. Not only that, Frankie, but your colour is wrong. I remember you as looking Mediterranean – like your name. But here you are, like a man turning up at his doctor with the jaundice moving in him. Well, I'll try some doctoring for a bit, and see can we not have ya going back a damn sight better than you've arrived. Here's a glass of tea. Don't worry – I've put a dash of Bushmills in it. Have a seat while I get ready."

Not quite elated by these words, Franklin looked around and remembered that the wall had once held numerous photos of Irish heroes, historical and mythical, as well as some portraits of Joyce and Yeats. These had all been replaced by some art that was presumably modern. The abstractions and cubes on display had a deadening effect on Franklin, and he attacked the tea more fiercely.

Tommy came in with a problem. "Eamon's coming over, Franklin, and maybe one or two others – we did not have the longest of notices from you. We'll have a few jars, but then afterwards, Eamon likes to get his molars around a good meat sandwich: maybe some beef or ham with mustard. And here have I not gone and slipped up. I have almost no bread in the house. Listen, Frankie. I'm just getting ready here. Would you mind nipping round to Fuzzy's and get a loaf of bread – white, if possible; thick slices, if you can. Sure it's a terrible indignity to heap onto an old pal; just arriving and being send on an errand. And for bread, of all things. I'm sorry, Frankie. Turn left when you go out, then left again, and Fuzzy's is the third shop down Talbot Street."

In the dark, it was less easy than Tommy had made it sound. But he assumed the small general store must be the right one. He stepped in. There were a few people waiting around.

"Is this Fuzzy's?" he asked.

There was some muffled sniggering.

"You better ask him," one of them said.

Franklin turned and saw the owner, black and fuzzy of head and beard.

"What did you say?" the owner asked.

Franklin saw the pickle he was in.

"Sorry, I meant Freddie's."

"Do I look like a Freddie?"

"Sorry. I'd like a white loaf of bread if you have one. Thickly sliced."

"Thickly sliced. Aren't you the particular one, now? Sean, go up there and see can ya find a white loaf with thick slices."

One of the other bystanders thought fit to add a little humour. "Hey, boys, di yas hear the one about the Scotsman that drove all the way from Glasgow to Dublin to find a decent loaf of bread?"

Franklin knew he had no option but to see it through and get out of there without further ruckus or damage. He paid for the bread and fumbled his way through the doorway to the sound of mocking laughter.

"Ah, well done, Frankie," said Tommy once he had returned. "Give us that loaf over here, and I'll put it away. It's a very handy shop, that. I don't think Fuzzy ever closes. Now, look, get yourself organised, and we'll slip over to *Lanigan's*. There's a couple of lads in there you'd want to meet. Heavy garglers, but I know you can go at your own pace. Especially during the season of Lent."

"*Lanigan's* still have live music? I seem to remember some enjoyable nights there listening to the ballads."

"Those days are gone; certainly from *Lanigan's*. Different scene now, Frank. Different tastes. The market for *The Foggy Dew* and *The Black Velvet Band* is not as strong as it was. But of course, there are places – there are dozens of places where you'll find traditional music. If you're keen on it we could check up where there might be some action for over the weekend. Haha. That OK, Action Man? I've a phone call to make while you put on your blue suede shoes. Five minutes and we're off."

They crossed Amiens Street and were turning into Talbot Street when Franklin received his next surprise.

"You know what day it is, of course, Frankie. The 25th of March."

"Ah, yes – you mean the Spring Equinox."

"No, that's some old pagan thing. And it was four days ago – Frankie, time to catch up! No, no, I meant the Feast of the Annunciation. Don't tell me you've forgotten!"

"I'm not as devout as I used to be, Tommy. But of course, now that you mention it – yes, the Annunciation: the Angel Gabriel and all that."

"Exactly, Frankie. Which is why I thought, on our way across to *Lanigan's*, we could nip in and catch the nine p.m. Mass in the pro-Cathedral. Eamon'll be there for sure. There's always a late evening Mass on major feasts like this. Half an hour or so, and then you'll enjoy your pint of Guinness even more."

It had been a long day for Franklin. He was tired. He could scarcely believe he was going to Mass after all these years. But he had no energy for an argument. In any case, what could he do – wait outside?

Mass had started when they went in. There was a fair crowd of worshippers, but Tommy knew where to find Eamon, and they slipped in beside him. He gave Franklin a brief nod, but no more, and did not break off his recitation of the Gloria to say hello.

The Gospel reading, from Luke, was still familiar to him, narrating the visit of Gabriel to Mary. The earlier reading from Isaiah he could not connect with until its final sentence: 'He shall eat butter and honey, that he may know to refuse evil and to choose good'. Bone-tired as he was, Franklin felt those words try to make a home in his mind.

Then right at the Consecration, as the altar boy's bell rang and the host was held aloft by the priest, Frankie felt a terrible, searing wrench around his liver. The pain shocked him but died away very quickly and left him no worse than breathless for a minute. He did not go up to receive communion, but the two brothers did. At the end, Eamon said he had to see the priest – it would only take a minute. Franklin felt a spasm of cramp in his left leg and left Tommy sitting while he took a stroll around the church. And as soon as he saw the various collection boxes affixed to the walls down the aisles, between the confessionals, he was struck again by a crystal-clear memory from his boyhood. In his own church, there were several such collection boxes – one said, 'The Holy Souls', and another, inscrutably, 'Saint Antony's Bread'. But one said, 'Children's Fund', and on Ash Wednesday evening, 1980, Franklin, going round to collect the hymn books left on the pews, noticed a small key in that box. A quick glance around, and he was shielding the box while he turned the key. The drawer slid open. There was quite a lot of coins, one five-pound note and about ten one-pound notes. Franklin slipped three of these out, closed the drawer and turned the key in the lock and, after a moment of hesitation, extracted the small key and put it in his pocket. On the Friday of that first week in Lent, at the altar boys' meeting, Father Cairns had announced that they feared some thief was operating in the church and asked the altar boys to be very watchful. If they saw anyone acting suspiciously, they should tell one of the priests immediately. Franklin was still hearing the words of the reading 'That he may know to refuse evil and choose good'. He had never reached that stage, he thought. What was he to do? Make a confession? But that seemed an impossibility.

He saw the brothers going down the centre aisle. From his pocket he pulled out two twenty-euro notes, folded them and was just about to push them into the 'Holy Souls' box, when a priest appeared at his elbow and whispered,

"Are you waiting to make your confession?"

This threw Franklin off balance. "No, thanks, Father," he muttered and went off, putting the euros back in his pocket.

At the church door, Tommy asked how his leg was. Franklin found it easy to agree, despite all the anticipation he had had, that the pub was not a good idea right then, and that a rest after a day's journey was much more fitting.

They went back to Tommy's. Eamonn fixed them beef sandwiches and strong tea, and they sat for a while exchanging news about themselves and their acquaintances.

On that subject, Tommy diplomatically enquired as to whether Franklin would like to have an escort during his stay. "Maybe not one of those heavenly girls from the Legion of Mary, but no sluts neither. Sadly, both Rachel and Nancy, who you were friendly with years ago, have both passed on to their reward. But God forgive me this holy night if I don't provide a nice bit of company for the best friend I have – in Scotland."

Franklin chuckled at this patter and its implied affection, but said he was slowing down a bit and would be glad of the rest from all things stressful, and right now, that included sex. But some company would be lovely.

"Indeed. I'm getting too old to run, meself. Who needs to run?"

"Depends who's chasing you."

As he sank into sleep, Franklin thought he heard the hymn, *I'll Sing a Hymn to Mary* coming from through the wall.

Chapter 10

Tommy's house, unimpressive from the outside steps, was one of those old, ramshackle dwellings that went on forever inside. Rooms, passages, alcoves, recesses like corridors – it was bewildering. Franklin slept late and when he'd washed, took a while to navigate to the kitchen. Not a sound. There was a note propped on the table. 'Gone for fish. Back by 12. T.' And added below, 'Gone to Mass. Back after 11. Eamonn'.

Mass again? thought Franklin. *God, I've landed in a monastery. At least he didn't waken me to go with him. These fellas have changed since we last met. I'm going to have to take that into account.* He sorted some cereal for himself, then managed to locate the toaster and fit two of the ultra-thick slices into the machine, obviously custom-built for Eamonn's needs. The Irish butter and the home-made marmalade were fresh and aromatic, as was the coffee. He began to feel more like himself for the first time in days. Eamonn returned first, hale and hearty and not at all subdued by having been to two Masses within twelve hours.

"Well rested, Frankie? I thought so. You know, the beds in this house are second to none. You'd go far and wide to find better beds. Tommy knew what he was doing when he took that consignment of beds. Years ago now, and of course, that was during the time of his tribulation. Thank God he's come through that, battered but unbruised, as it says in *The Pilgrim's Progress*. I know he was saying last night that he's slowing down, but, he's a better man. No doubt, on your visit, you'll be having a few late nights on the town, and good luck to ya. But Tommy won't be seeing it through with you – through the night, I mean. He's always home before midnight these days. As I am meself. But don't you worry, we'll make sure you have as much Irish hospitality as your liver can withstand. Sure, the city is full of young desperadoes and scallywags, even if some of them talk Korean. I know you've visited us often, but maybe you haven't quite seen as much as you could. I don't mean silly tourist things like that Blarney Stone racket in Cork. But the island has some truly fascinating secrets. Don't know if you're up to secrets, Frankie. You can sometimes get more out of a secret exploration than you can from ten pints of Guinness."

Eamon's relentless chatter would have gone on had not the sound of Tommy returning broken up the discussion. Tommy appeared in the kitchen doorway carrying two large boxes. The tang of fresh fish was overpowering.

"I'll put more ice on these, and then I'll be with you."

Franklin looked quizzically at Eamonn. "Seems like an awful lot of fish. You must love it."

"We do. But Tommy helps with a local food bank. 'Fish on Friday' is a slogan that goes back to the start of the Catholic Church. No longer commanded, of course, but still lots of people keep to the custom of having fish for their dinner on Fridays. But you go to the merchants to get it fresh on Friday. They know Tommy and his work for the hungry, and he gets a good price."

"Good thinking, Eamonn. Smart enterprise. So, he's making a few bucks while he's cutting people's costs."

"Not exactly. It's not an enterprise. Tommy pays upfront. It's charity work. I'm still a bit of a rapscallion when I get the chance, but me brother, he's the saint of the North Strand."

At this point Tommy came in, chuckling, and said,

"What a calamity it would be if you lived in Dublin and didn't like fish."

"Eamonn was just telling me about your work for the poor, Tommy. It's fantastic."

"You know, Frankie, there's a great little local baker's not far from here, and sometimes after I've got the fish deliveries ready, I'll call in on him and talk him out of a few loaves of bread. Then when I hand over the goods, it's loaves and fishes! You know – like in that crazy Gospel story where Jesus multiplies the coupla loaves and a few fish into enough to feed five thousand. I find the picture very amusing – Tommy the new

Messiah. And I tell the people at the food bank. They laugh, too. When you're doing good, Franklin, everybody smiles."

This is turning into the holiday of the loaves, though Franklin. Tommy went on,

Tommy went on. "Right, here's the plan. I have this work to do now. So I've asked Catherine – you remember my daughter – to take you over to Howth for the afternoon. Tim, her man, Tim Reilly, will be there too, and they'll bring their youngster along. You'll love him. You'll have a lovely time over there. They said they'd be here about one, and of course, the Dart train is only across the road, so no need for the car. Eamonn, d'you want to nip down to the *Wok On Inn* and get us a takeaway for lunch. Just for the three of us. They'll not want any Chinese food. Sweet and sour chicken OK with you, Frankie?"

Over lunch, Tommy explained that his family would meet Franklin at Howth Station. He gave Franklin Catherine's number and said to phone her when his train was on its way. So at one fifteen, Franklin was moving out of Connolly Street station on the twenty-five-minute ride out to that strange looping peninsula that formed the northern end of Dublin Bay. Remembering to smile, he waved to Catherine, whom he recognised immediately. She bounded over and gave him a big hug. Tim followed and they shook hands. Their son had a serious look on his face, neither welcoming nor resentful, but alert and intelligent.

Franklin was waiting for one of the parents to introduce him, but neither did. They were waiting for him, it seemed.

"Hello. Shall I call you Uncle Frank?"

"That's fine by me. And who might you be?"

"My name is Montgomery Reilly. And please don't call me Monty."

"You're right – terrible name, Monty. Not fit for a soldier."

"Ha-ha – that's a good one, Uncle Frank. Did you just make that up?"

"I was a professional comedian for years."

"Yes, but is your name short for Francis?"

"No, it is not. My first name is Franklin."

"Ooh, that's a good name. I would rather call you Uncle Franklin if that's all right."

"It is. Franklin Gaddarini is pleased to make the acquaintance of Montgomery Reilly."

"That is some name. Should I call you Uncle Franklin Gaddarini?"

"That's very long. Life's hard enough. Let's settle for Uncle Franklin."

This dialogue threatened to go on forever. It amused Catherine and Tim. It astonished Franklin that the boy could pick up so quickly on the reference to Field-Marshall Montgomery. It served to begin a bond between them from the very outset.

Tim pointed out the way they might take a woodland walk up the hill. Catherine managed most of the chat, telling Tim tales about the Franklin of old, and how she was sure he was still just as much a livewire as the time when he got up on the stage of the *Old Shieling* – once Dublin's *Grand Ole Opry* – and sang *It Ain't Me, Babe*.

Franklin laughed, flattered by such a dramatic memory. He tried to recall when last he had sung anything live and simply could not remember.

They stopped at a hillside café, and Montgomery advised having the strawberry sundae, the best of its kind in Ireland. But the adults played safe with cappuccinos and enjoyed watching Montgomery deal expertly with the strawberry sundae. It was all very pleasant, no prying, no questions. Tim was fond of trivia and what he said Radio 2 called factoids and managed to pass on some information about things like 'a shrimp's heart is located in its head' and 'elephants can't jump'. Catherine was used to it. But a question came when Montgomery returned after going over to view Ireland's Eye through a telescope.

He asked, "Uncle Franklin, do you mind telling me what you do for a living? I bet it's very interesting."

Franklin was caught off guard. So much for thinking on his feet, he replied, "I'm a bus driver."

There was silence, and enough space for Franklin to think of a modification to an answer that had shocked all three of his companions.

"It is an interesting story, as you rightly guessed, Montgomery. I have a friend who works for a hospital that looks after sick and injured children, and he has a small company that take these unfortunate kids to the seaside or to castles and places of interest. He runs three buses, and a month ago his main driver, Alex, fell down the stairs of the bus and broke both his legs. Couldn't work, obviously – can't drive a bus with no legs."

"A bus with no legs – that's funny," Montgomery chortled.

"When I heard about this, I just thought, I have plenty of time on my hands just now. I could help. So twice a week, I do a bus run; take sick kids to places like Girvan or St Andrew's or Edinburgh. I do have other work, of course, but it's boring office stuff, and frankly—" He paused and Montgomery nodded and laughed. Franklin continued. "I enjoy the bus-driving more. Wouldn't do as a full-time job, money's poor. Anyway, that's me. What work do you hope to do?"

"I can't say, I'm afraid. I'm sworn to secrecy. But I'm afraid I must tell you this – it will not be a bus driver. The bus drivers in Ireland I've come across are all rather untidy. And they never want to discuss things."

While his parents had a friendly little talk with their son on the themes of equality and snobbery, Franklin finally managed to catch his breath. He was thankful now that he had not been in touch with the Irish branch of the family for several years, and so he could get away with several untruths, as required. He reminded himself to keep smiling, still a very unnatural state for Franklin.

After some pleasant sight-seeing, the afternoon was ending, and they made their way downhill towards the station.

But once there, Catherine took Franklin's arm and said, "You're coming with us. Just for tea. Then I'm to take you over to Dad's place around seven. He said that'll give him time to finish his work and clear the way to attend to you. Our car's here. I'm afraid you'll have to put up with Lord Snooty for another couple of hours. We're over in Phibsborough. Not far from the Zoo."

Near the car, Tim almost stood on a snail. "Oops, just missed it. Did you know that a snail can sleep for three years?"

"I did," Franklin lied, loving the look on Montgomery's face. "Everybody knows that."

On the drive back, Franklin surprised everyone, himself most of all, by breaking into an unaccompanied version of *It Ain't Me, Babe*, which he was alleged to have made famous many years before. He didn't get past the first verse, however, the lyrics being tricky to remember at that length of time. But he was roundly applauded, and perhaps that marked the entry of Franklin Gaddarini into the Reilly family.

They had an elegant, modern house, clearly not following Catherine's father's example. They were a modern Irish couple, who tried to sift the good from their history and culture, and promote it when they could, and leave the rest to fade. Both were religious and practising Catholics, they told Franklin outright, but they had no sympathy for the authoritarians in the Church who had lorded it over the Irish population for centuries. Even aside from the terrible priest-paedophile scandals of recent times, they saw many practices that could be consigned to the dustbin.

Catherine was a pharmacist, and Tim was a teacher of French and Italian. In addition to boy-wonder –Tim's sarcastic phrase – Montgomery, they had a sixteen-year-old daughter called Niamh, who was being educated at a private religious academy.

Montgomery added, "So you won't have to meet her on this occasion."

They had a lovely meal of smoked salmon and salad, with potatoes boiled in their jackets. And never for a second was Franklin made to feel inferior or different, the supposed rough-and-tumble bus-driver from Glasgow being thoroughly worthy of his place at their table and their fireside.

Franklin felt he should be cautious about making a fool of himself, but he asked Tim, "Is teaching French a good job, then, Tim? I mean, do you get a lift out of it, or is it like most other jobs – just a job?"

"I do get a lift, Franklin, yes. Of course it varies from class to class and from year to year. But the Irish take to French like a duck to ether."

"A duck to ether, eh? Well! Never heard that one."

"They're better at Italian – remember that many places here still have the Mass in Latin. Of course, fewer and fewer students are choosing languages nowadays."

Six o'clock came and went, and Montgomery had an evening swimming lesson. Tim would take care of that, and Catherine would drive Franklin across to Tommy's. Franklin felt like a soldier whose wounds were finally starting to heal.

Chapter 11

Catherine used the short journey as an opportunity to bring Franklin up to date on a few matters.

"I'm glad you got on so well with Tim. He's such a lovely man. He's a man of ideas, Tim, not like you, Franklin – I hope you don't mind me saying so. He's just the kind of father our children need, they being rather precocious – too much so, for me, at times. But Tim is never fazed, never knocked off course. Last time I saw you, I was twenty-three. Now I'm thirty-eight. You must be forty-nine. Time isn't kind to any of us, but you look like time has been using you as a football. Maybe you're still trying to live as you did when you were young. When you could keep up with the pace. My dad and Uncle Eamonn were the same, of course. But they've learned. They've changed and adapted, and maybe already you notice a difference in them. I just wanted to alert you to that, so you're not disappointed or too surprised. Fifteen years is the longest you've been away from here, and we've often talked about you. So, for my dad to get a phone call on Monday saying you were coming next day – all hell broke loose. He would never, ever have put you off. He should have said,

'Whoa, give us a few days and we'll have a lovely visit set out for you'. So, to arrive like this, Franklin, makes me worry a bit. It makes me think you had to leave in a hurry."

They had reached Amiens Street by now, but Catherine pulled up and parked two hundred yards from the house.

"I know you thought of me at times. For a year or two, I hoped I'd get a letter. I don't suppose you're much of a letter-writer, though. But I couldn't play Maid Marian waiting for Robin Hood to return. Remember you used to like that game, Frankie – Robin and Marian. A mere fantasy, but a lovely one. But now? Franklin, I hope you have someone you can talk to. I mean about the important things. Someone you can utterly trust. I know you're living with someone. But when I look at you, I don't think she's the one. Forgive me, this sounds so arrogant. I've never met her. I just think that there is someone that you need to share things with, and you haven't found that person. It could be another woman; it could be a priest; it could even be a drinking buddy; it could be Tommy. Not only have you not found the person, to me you don't seem to have even started to look. Something inside you is blocking any progress. Maybe it's to do with your father. Is he still regarded as 'disappeared'?"

Franklin was silent, staring at the ground This was a subject he did not talk about.

But Catherine was strong, and persevered. "Tell me what you think happened. Please, Franklin."

"My father is not dead. For unclear reasons, he left us suddenly and returned to his native village in Italy. He is still in Italy. When it's time for him to return or contact us, he'll know."

It was almost recited, and Catherine recognised that. It was a version Franklin cobbled and learned for his own protection.

She only replied, "Right, let's get in. Watch the step – it's a high one."

Franklin began to worry, and in his head he felt afraid. Catherine's affectionate peck on the cheek helped a little. As they walked slowly towards the house, Franklin began to see how life could differ. In Glasgow, he ordered Jem to go and find a glazier; in Dublin, his uncle told him to go and buy *a loaf*. In Glasgow, an afternoon free was spent in the *Ewe and Lamb*; here he had just spent an afternoon wheezing up grassy slopes and viewing the scenic delights of Ireland's Eye from Howth Head. In Glasgow, everyone was looking out for themselves; here his cousin was dedicated to feeding the hungry. These were different ways of living. As for going to night Mass instead of a bar...

"The explorers return," cried Eamonn, "and with a bit of red in their cheeks. Good enough!"

Franklin took a shower and joined the other three in the big room beside the kitchen, where a large, deep table served a multitude of purposes. Near Eamonn was a plate of ham sandwiches, thick cut, and there was also a tray with cakes and biscuits. Before he could say a word, Tommy had poured him some strong, dark tea, and asked would he take a bite. Having eaten less than two hours before, Franklin declined. Eamonn smiled. But Franklin reached for a slice of fruit cake. Tommy smiled. They nattered away for ages about everything and nothing, although Montgomery and his prowess remained the subject of admiring conversation for a good stretch. About eight o'clock, came a triple bang on the door.

"That'll be the rent man," opined Eamonn. "I've told him and told him we've bought the house, but he keeps coming back looking for rent money. He's soft in the head. Maybe he does it as a hobby."

But a rather raspy female voice was heard, and Eamonn amended his opinion immediately.

"It's ould Molly. She lives round the back. I mean up the next street, not round our back. She's a card. I don't think ya ever met her before, Frankie."

Greetings were boisterous and involved much pummelling and throwing back of heads and all that kind of thing. Molly hugged Franklin tightly, as if a lost brother. She had no sooner sat at the table with them than Tommy placed a bottle of Jameson in front of her, and a glass.

"God love yez this blessed night," were her first intelligible words, as she unscrewed the bottle top deftly and splashed out a measure. Tommy and Catherine declined, being on soft drinks. Eamonn had a bottle of Remy-Martin beside him, and Franklin, now, kept to Harp lager. Molly had a tale to tell about a Japanese man who had moved in above her, and who surely had his eye on her. 'Or maybe both eyes – it was hard for Molly to tell. Later Franklin was to discover that this was certainly untrue, but that Molly liked to alert the two brothers that there might be a rival come on the scene. She fussed a lot over Eamonn, and made a fuss of his remarks, while keeping much cooler towards Tommy. But it was Tommy she had her sights on. Catherine told Franklin about this drama later, but Franklin saw something of it for himself.

"Now, before we get any drunker," announced Tommy, "let's have a game at something. The great thing about dominoes is that it's easy to remember the rules. With cards you always get arguments about the rules, but not dominoes. So here we are."

And he tipped a box of dominoes onto the cover and gave them a face-down shuffle.

He looked up. "Wait. There's five of us. The rules say maximum four players."

"So here comes the rule book right away," cried Molly.

Catherine insisted she would not play, or maybe later, and Eamonn suggested she be referee and look out for any cheating. Tommy and Eamonn were the experts and won a few games between them before Molly took the fifth game, after a lot of effing and blinding. "Where's my feckin double four," she would say, to be scolded by Tommy and advised by Eamonn that you didn't let players know which dominoes you had.

Franklin was now the only one without a win. He decided that the Harp lager, pleasant enough, did not have the kick to take him where he needed to be. So he excused himself to Molly, who fluttered her eyes for almost twenty seconds, and took a dollop of Jameson, hoping thus to call in his domino muse. And it worked. He won the next two games. Catherine then mooted that his earlier form had been so bad, that now winning games only when he had consumed glasses of whiskey rendered his wins invalid. There was a hubbub. Franklin pointed out that Eamonn's Remy-Martin bottle was quite the worse for wear, so he too would need to forfeit his early victories.

Just after ten o'clock, Franklin feared that the whiskey was causing him to hear things, because Eamonn seemed to have said, "Right. Time for the Rosary. Well, listen, we have guests. So why don't we make it just one decade of the Rosary."

"Would you ever get me pillow?" asked Molly, and a plump pillow was placed in front of her, which she quickly slid onto, all the while holding level her glass of whiskey. She placed it carefully on the table between the double-five and the three-one. From a pocket she took out a little purse containing her rosary beads. So did the others, who knelt and leaned on their chairs, and Catherine slipped a spare rosary to Franklin.

Tommy said, "It'll be the Joyful mysteries, and the first Joyful mystery is The Annunciation."

I'm never going to escape from this Annunciation, thought Franklin, as Tommy got the prayers underway with the *Our Father*.

The whole service was over in ten minutes, and Molly went straight back to her glass, though only after she had fastened the button on her rosary purse and snucked it away.

Eamonn turned on the television and they chatted across its inanities. This did not please Molly, a rabid fan of anything lowbrow. She was Dublin before Reconstruction.

"I like a chance to see the TV. My TV is not working."

"How's that?" asked Franklin.

"It switches itself off just when I'm at some good bit. Sometimes it comes back on by itself, sometimes it doesn't. The other night, EastEnders is minutes from the finish, when bapp! Black screen! I pray to Our Lord Jesus Christ and to his Holy Mother, but even they can't restore the picture. Eamonn, I wonder would you ever take a run along sometime and have a look at it for me?"

"No, no, Molly, wrong department. Tommy here is the technician in this household, and he's your man for sulky TV sets. Tommy'll have a look, not to worry."

"I will, Molly, over the weekend. And if I can't sort it, I'll check out who is the patron saint of television, and you can pray to him too. Speaking of the weekend, Franklin, now that we've sort of caught up with you, we're trying to fix a wee night – you know, song and craic and good cheer and maybe a little jug o' punch. Not too many, but I have got in touch with a few who you'll be glad to see again."

"That's terrific, Tommy. Just what I was hoping."

"One thing I'll have to tell you. Our brother, Robert, will be there. He called today to say he's coming over on Saturday morning. From Kildare."

"I didn't know you had another brother. The times I've been over, I don't think I ever met him."

"No, no, you wouldn't have. He's younger than us. But that's not it. He's, well, he's a bit different. A bit eccentric is a good word you don't hear enough of these days. Yes, he's an eccentric rather than a psychotic, for example."

Eamonn found this remark especially funny and wheezed away with laughter.

Tommy continued his explanation. "He's not very sociable, and of course, many Irish people regard that as a great weakness of character. What is life without a ceilidh – that kind of attitude. Robert doesn't do ceilidhs. He doesn't do weddings or christenings. He doesn't really do people. He's coming up to the city on some business thing, and I mentioned you were here, and we were having a small gathering on Saturday night. And to my surprise, he said, 'Very well. I'll be there by seven.'"

"All very interesting," said Franklin." I'm looking forward to seeing him."

"Yes, of course, but maybe I'll give you just a little tutorial beforehand, on some of the do's and don'ts with Robert."

"My Lord, Tommy, now you're making him sound dangerous. Franklin, just so long as you treat Robert as the Chief, you'll be all right. Unlike us, he has some education. No need for tutorials. Tommy tried tutorials with me once and look where that got me!"

Tommy and Eamonn laughed at one another.

They all assumed Molly was caught up in the television, but she added, "I met Robert long ago. Years ago. He asked me to come outside, and he would show me the stars."

No one seemed ready to ask the next question. So Tommy asked Catherine would she go and bring in the soup. All back over to the table. Tomato soup and warm rolls at eleven p.m. They all stooped forward and attacked the soup like starved convicts.

Molly had come back out of her daydream, and said, "I see that nobody here smokes cigarettes. That's wonderful. I gave up last year when I finally couldn't afford the astrocosmical prices they were asking. Did you ever smoke yourself, Frank?"

"I did, long ago. I gave up about twenty years ago – and they weren't nearly as expensive then."

"Did you feel it's done you good to stop?"

"I dunno. Not really," answered Franklin in an odd moment of *in vino veritas*. "My drinking increased when I stopped smoking, I remember that."

"How right you are there, Frankie. Bejaysus, if it's not one thing, it's another. Tommy, that's delicious soup. Where did you get the tomatoes from?"

Chapter 12

Franklin opened the window of his room to look out onto Amiens Street by night. He got a surprise. He was one floor above ground, but it was pitch-dark down there. He heard some sounds, like somebody raking through rubbish. Then he heard a tapping sound like a hammer would make. He strained to see, but only some shapes came to him. He realised he was facing into somewhere at the back or side of the building, not its front. This house was so strangely assembled. He closed the window as the tapping continued. Who's out among the rubbish with a hammer at midnight?

He thought back to a holiday he had taken just a year before. There was sunshine and light, sparkling water, lively music and good-looking people everywhere. He wondered if where he was could be called a holiday.

He had a strange dream. He was in the dock in an old-fashioned courtroom. A wigged judge was facing him. He was conducting the case and his lips were moving, but Franklin could not hear him. While the case was going on, different people were moving around, entering and leaving, whispering and pointing.

Then the judge's slow sonorous voice became more audible. "Quentin Gabardini, the jury have not returned, and so I am going to proceed with the case. This was a crime of great aggression, and only the profound skills of the surgeon saved the victim from a brutal death. Central to the case has been the weapon – alleged to be a claw-hammer by which the serious assault was carried out. But as it turns out, the hammer had a claw at each side of its head, and so cannot meaningfully be called a hammer in the usual sense of the word. Although you were present at the attack at the time, and although some forensic evidence weighs strongly against you, I have not been convinced that you are guilty, as charged, of serious assault and attempted murder. You may step down. You are free to go. Don't come back."

Franklin, dumbstruck, moved down towards the exit, but at the door a uniformed arm was stretched out to block his way.

"I am the sergeant-at-arms. You can't leave yet."

"But the judge has just said I could. He said I'm free."

"Yes, well, in this court that's for the jury to decide. The jury's coming back soon. Any minute now. And then we'll see who's free and who's not."

Franklin looked around, but he was trapped, literally, in a corner, and the sergeant's eyes were hard. He thought if the jury heard about his previous troubles, he would be doomed – he would never be free. The general hubbub of the place suddenly quietened down, and the sound of footsteps of people was all that could be heard. Franklin knew it was the returning jury. He felt utterly terrified.

Franklin came awake with this swirling around his mind, and tears on his face. Of relief? Of terror? He could not tell. He tried for a while to keep the dream from dissolving, so that he could try to understand it. As he became more conscious, he heard again the tune and words of a hymn that he knew – 'Hail, Glorious Saint Patrick, dear saint of our isle…' It was 1.20 a.m. Who on earth could be singing? It must be a recording, possibly from the same wretched album as the previous night. He was awake and alert briefly, and felt a bolt of memory strike him: what penance had Mr Patrick sentenced him to? He could check his emails on his phone but decided against it. A long time passed before he got back to sleep.

He rose at nine a.m. and went through to the big room. There, again, was a message propped against a biscuit box. Tommy informed him, that it being Saturday, they were both busy all day until around four p.m. He had the day to himself, and Tommy suggested he just go freewheeling around the city to any parts, especially in the centre, he remembered with interest or affection. Tommy added that his sister, Jacqueline, had called and would love to see him if he had time. She worked next to St Stephen's Green. And he left her phone number.

The note ended with: 'I promise we will go out to a bar tonight. So don't take too much in the afternoon. Or in the morning, for that matter! And remember – things have changed. T.'

Luckily, it was a fine, spring day, and the heavy overcoat was not required. He sauntered down to O'Connell Street, crowded and busy as always, and over into Henry Street and chuckled at the timeless cries and old jokes of the market sellers as they plied their wares. A man with green hair offered him, for fifteen euros, a T-shirt with a full print of Patrick Pearse on the front. When he insisted it was 'an original', Franklin couldn't help laughing and willingly paid up.

He went on into Mary Street and then turned down towards the Quays. He sauntered back along the river, now universally lined with restaurants and bars. The old cafes had been swamped out by the big conglomerates, who seemed to have a hand in every hospitality business in the city. Across O'Connell Bridge again and down onto Eden Quay, even more hip and booming, young men and women looking so good at their outdoor tables and filling the air gently with the silver thread of Dublinspeak. He had been on his feet for more than an hour and slipped with relief onto one of the empty chairs.

"Could I have a double macchiato with two sugars please?" he asked the waiter.

"Comment, monsieur?"

"A double macchiato – you know, a small espresso but with milk - and two lumps of sugar; thanks."

The waiter remained in place. He was puzzled, possibly by Franklin's Glasgow accent. "You are from somewhere? You are not from here, sir? *Vous venez du Nord?*"

"I am from Scotland – Glasgow. I've been here a dozen times and more. Where are you from yourself, by the way? Not here either, I suspect."

The waiter shrugged and pointed at the sign above: *Le Bistro Irlandais*.

"I am from Lyons, thank you, sir. I will fetch your coffee."

He did, and now that Franklin had stopped walking, he felt a little more able to think, and he tried to put a bit of understanding into the last few days, for he thought he had been a continuous helter-skelter all week since the Sunday armchair incident, which seemed so distant now, and yet still had its claws in his mind. As he sat there, he began to feel how cluttered that mind had become. When he started to consider one issue, soon another one edged it offstage. He tried to apply his mind to the whole connection with Mr Patrick and his strange brotherhood. He puzzled for the hundredth time about the women he had introduced to the brotherhood. He had seen no signs that any of the women came to even the slightest harm in their dealings with the old blokes. His phone already contained a message from him – no question – that he would need to answer and deal with. It would probably be some kind of task or even mission. Just as he was about to check his emails, his mind bustled in and placed a different situation in front of him: he needed to find out more about Robert – the brother – before he arrived, because he had a corner of his memory which was trying to remind him why he should be wary of Robert. Then as he was trying to sort these out, a third matter arose, and urgently.

Tommy had advised against drinking much, but right at that moment a pint and a couple of whiskies sounded overwhelmingly attractive. In this state of mind, he was simply unable to begin sorting out the mess he was in. Of course, part of that problem was that Franklin had not yet truly admitted that there was any mess to begin with. So this bout of introspection and self-assessment ended with a familiar cop-out: *I'm on holiday here; I'm taking a much-needed break; life's hard enough.* And he got up, dusted himself down, picked up his new T-shirt and restarted his tour. He crossed the river and took the bend round towards Grafton Street, very busy with up-market shoppers and bustling with young executives and rich-looking bankers. As he walked, a little clarity and order came into his thoughts.

My life is in pieces. It's in fragments. A lot of the fragments are interesting. Some aren't. Some are nasty – dangerous. But I steer a way through them. I stop to enjoy the tasty fragments, the happy events. I'm an optimist. I don't stumble when some little obstacle gets in the way. On I go – Franklin Gaddarini on his way through life. It's all a lot of twists and turns. You don't know what's round the corner. You win some, you lose some. I'm not claiming to be invincible. I'm not indestructible. But I'm hard to knock over. I go along with much confidence…

He thudded into a man waiting at the pavement, nearly knocking him into the road. He apologised, made sure the man was unhurt, and carried on. He thought to himself, *Yes – hard to knock over; might have killed that man.* He took the street right round by Trinity and arrived at the river again. He crossed and turned onto Eden's Quay. He recognised *Lanigan's* pub, went in and sat down with his back against a padded seat.

Immediately a waiter came over, wearing a sash of green, white and gold. "Good afternoon, sir. Would you like a drink?"

"A pint of Harp, please."

"I'm sorry, sir, we do not have Harp on draught. What about some Guinness?"

"No, I'm looking for something cooler – a beer or lager."

"We have Kronenbourg, Moretti, Heineken…"

"Your uniform is pretty Irish all right, but you have no Irish lager?"

"Not on draught, sir. The Kronenbourg is an excellent cool lager, sir."

"Very well. A pint of Kronenbourg and a large Jameson's with a jug of water on the side."

"Very good, sir," whispered the waiter, backing away and, but for the sash, looking and sounding more like Jeeves than Joyce. Never mind – this was more like it. The drinks were set before him immediately, and he dived in. He felt the ropes inside him slackening just a little.

An older fellow nearby called over, "The first one's always the best! Isn't that the case now?"

"Indeed it is, old-timer," said Franklin, "and we rarely stop at the one, eh?"

"You're so right there. I find that myself, and then after the fourth, I'm only wishing I could go back to the first again. Well, you're right. Not only that, but you're a philosopher, no doubt. Am I right? You're a philosopher from Scotland, taking a little break in the land of the leprechauns."

Franklin finished his drinks and ordered refills and a pint of Guinness for his new companion.

"Now, old fella," he said. "You can repay me that by giving me a wee bit of advice. I'm over staying with two of my cousins, down at Amiens Street, and tonight they're taking me out drinking. The city has changed a lot since I was last here, twelve years ago. Are there still good Irish bars to be found for a night out on a Saturday? If there are any, something tells me you'll be the boy that knows them."

"Lots of people make the same complaint – that Dublin has changed for the worse. It's true that styles are always changing, and here, a lot of the change is just show and froth. What I would say is, decide what it is you're looking for – be precise about that. And then go and find it. Chances are, you will find it in Dublin. Now as to Saturdays, there are all kinds of options, depending on your taste. There are quiet bars, though not many, sports bars with huge screens, jukebox bars for the kids, drinking bars for the fighters; you wouldn't go there. Political bars for people that like to argue, and music bars. Now as to music, there is some pop stuff and some cokaroky, I believe it's called. *The Lower Deck*, as you would know if you used to come over, was a mainstay of the ballads. Now its's a cokaroky. But there are open mic sessions, where you might contribute a song or two yourself, and there are ballad sessions – many, many of them still. What's your pick? Sorry, my name is Gabriel. How d'ye do?"

"Ah – Franklin is the name. Yes, probably some traditional ballad music would be wonderful. I used to love the *Old Shieling* at Raheny, and the *Abbey Tavern* in Howth, and there was an open mic place twenty years ago called *The Limelight*, I think – can't remember where that was."

"Right, right – let me think. *O'Donogues* is a favourite, in Baggot Street, five minutes from St Stephen's Green. 'Twas Michael Collins's drinking haunt. It does get very busy and crowded, though. But if you're staying down by Amiens Street, sure you have a fine place just minutes from there in Talbot Street. Probably new to you, but I hear it's fine music there. It's called *The Celt* – music every night, and it has a sister restaurant next door. The other one I'm considering is *Darkey Kelly's* near Christchurch Cathedral. It was once a brothel. Maybe still is. You might get lucky, heh-heh – you and your two cousins: Jesus, that'd be fun. Ye might get more than yez can handle! Dorcas or Darkey Kelly was the madame of the brothel. Take care, though, if you're superstitious. Darkey was burned at the stake in 1761 for killing five guests. It's not far out – it's on a bend in Fishamble Street, near the castle. It's getting home I'm thinkin' of. You'd want to make sure you get a taxi. You wouldn't walk from there to Amiens Street on a Saturday night with a bellyful of apples and plums. No, I'd say maybe *The Celt* is your best bet."

Franklin thanked him. They chatted for a while. Franklin rose to go and thanked Gabriel once again.

"Do you follow the horses?" Gabriel asked.

"No. Well, now and again. I used to bet quite regularly. Kinda lost interest, recently."

"I can see that. Yes. Well, anyway, there's a horse running today at Leopardstown, in the 4.15. Name of *The Carlow Patrician*. I hear he's been quietly brought along and prepared for this race. You might get around 10/1. I'm not a regular punter myself, but when this fella passes me a tip, I give it a shot, and it wins more often than it loses. That's the worst I can say, and I know you'll be thinking that I'm giving you the same old patter tipsters always produce. It's up to you. Be sure to look for me any time you're back in here."

"Ok, it's worth a little interest. I'll just write the name down."

"No! Don't do that. That's bad luck. Write it down on a betting slip when you get to a bookie's. Not before."

Franklin decided to continue along the quays towards the docks rather than get bombarded with fancy shops and stores. He followed the river around and came upon a quite extraordinary sight. A man was sitting on a two-seater couch backed against a large shed, so that he was facing out to the water. The man had a rug over his legs up to his waist. But his hair was what caught the eye. Long and white, it wreathed and twisted its ways upwards, outwards and backwards into points. *Surely*, Franklin thought, *that must be with some powerful gel or hairspray*. But when he got closer, he saw how the strands of hair moved slowly like wraiths, a life-form in their own right.

The man's hands were resting on his lap, but he raised one when he saw Franklin. "Hello! Hello! Are you a sailor just come ashore offa one of the boats?"

"No, I'm not. I'm taking a stroll in this fine, spring weather."

"That's all very well, but if you're not a sailor newly come ashore, then what are you? "

"I'm just a visitor. I'm here on a visit."

"Ah. Well, pass along, then. I'm looking out for a sailor."

"Ok. Good luck with that. Nice to meet you."

"Take care on the water. And keep a lookout for my brother. He looks exactly like me. But he's a devilish sort of man. Be careful. He's near here somewhere, and he'll take you by surprise."

"Well, listen, pal, I have to say you took me by surprise yourself. I'm starting to feel like that guy long ago who went on that long trip and met all sorts of creatures. Can't recall his name. I would not be surprised to hear that he's met you along the way."

"I've met a few travellers in my time, that's true. In fact that's what my life now is – listening to travellers tell their tales. That's why I asked were you a sailor just come ashore from some voyage."

"Well, sorry again, pal, but I feel more like I've just started on some weird voyage rather than just coming off of one."

"Yes. Well, if you go to sea, come and tell me about it. "

There was a branch of Paddy Power's beside the station, and Franklin went in. He managed to recall the name of the horse, and wrote it on a slip, adding below the name, '50 euros to win. Leop. 4.15.' At the teller's counter, he passed over the slip and a fifty euro note, and he smiled, and the teller seemed puzzled as to his smiling. Franklin looked around. There were about fifteen people in the shop. Not one had a smile on his face. *Did Paddy Power know about this?* he chuckled to himself, which drew a few looks. Clearly this Scot was insane.

Chapter 13

Rafferty's Bar, just off Capel Street, is where Tommy, Eamonn and Robert had taken Franklin, in preference to Gabriel's suggestions. Its mix of warmth and darkness appealed to him right away, and he insisted on buying the first round, even though he felt a little trepidation about asking the saturnine Robert, what he would drink.

"Vodka and tomato juice is what I usually start with," was the reply, containing a hint of more thrilling choices to follow later.

They bantered and gargled, and slowly the talk moved from the present to the past to the historical past and back again, and Franklin felt there was a soothing balance to their group. Robert brought a quality of gravity that kept Franklin's scale from dipping too low. Someone mentioned horse racing and suddenly Franklin was reminded of his bet.

He became excited. "Eamonn, that man I met today, Gabriel, he gave me a tip for a horse, and I put a few quid – a few euros – on it. Can you find out how it ran?"

Eamonn spoke to a man in a trilby who came over.

"Now tell me this and tell me no more. D'ye want to know all the results, or was it just the one race?"

"Yes. The 4.15. Leopardstown. My horse is… wait a minute now, the slip's here. Yes, *Act of Contrition*. In the 4.15."

"No luck, pal. No, the 4.15 was won by *Carlow Patrician*. At 12/1."

Franklin saw at once the horrible mistake he had made. He had misremembered *Carlow Patrician*, which he now recognised as the tip passed on by Gabriel. Act of Contrition, he thought. *Isn't that funny now?*

"D'you know if any horse ran by the name of *Act of Contrition*?"

"I could if I was to go online and check the Racing Post full results. But I can't right now. And to be honest, I've never heard of a horse of that name, though certainly if there was one, it would surely be Irish."

"Maybe I'll get my stake back if it's a non-runner."

"Yes. You do have some chance of that."

This dampener did not last long. Franklin's eye was drawn several times to a woman a few tables along, sitting side-on to him. Her hair was long and lustrous, and the profile of her face was quite striking.

Franklin looked that way more and more, until Tommy said, "Nice lady. Dymphna is her name. Been coming here for many years. Used to sing regularly. Now, only very occasionally. Franklin, I'm not sure if you're even listening to me. If not, pay attention. She's a lovely woman. She's single. But she's also blind. I'll be honest, Franklin. I could see you really messing up her life. So, don't go there. Just don't."

Franklin pretended to be uninterested, and when he and Eamonn went to the toilet and came back, they changed seats, as if Franklin was saying, "See – I don't need to look at her."

At nine o'clock sharp, a few bold chords struck up, a fiddle whined into action, and a deep voice broke right into 'Well I'm a Rover, Seldom Sober...' and the game was on. After joyful applause, the pace and the theme were maintained with 'And it's All for me Grog, Me jolly, jolly grog...' A guitar, a banjo, a fiddle and a borann were the mainstay, and a mandolin, another guitar and a melodeon all got turns, and the crowd was highly pleased.

After about eight in a row without a break, they finally concluded their treatment of the theme of drink and settled into some much quieter and cultivated ballads, and not all of them Irish. The guitarist announced that later he hoped a few would come up and treat them to a song.

Franklin glanced at Robert, trying to imagine this basilisk of a face breaking into song and wondering what that song might be. He had not managed to get very far with Robert, but his aloofness was not snobbery. He was just a quiet man who felt no urge to speak for the sake of convention. In fact, he was a deeply considerate man with a dry humour to match.

He took hold of Franklin's arm and told him a little story. "When I was younger, I spent some time in a monastery. I thought I might have a vocation to the religious life. I spent some time with the Benedictines. I left, of course, or I wouldn't be on this third vodka, at least not in this bar. Anyway, there was a lot of time spent in prayer, and at that period I was quite addicted to cigarettes. I found it extremely hard to go for an hour without a smoke. Sometimes when I was at prayer, I lit up a cigarette and smoked while I was praying. This troubled me, and I asked my confessor about it. 'Is it a sin to smoke while I'm praying, Father?' And he said the way to see it is to ask yourself, 'Am I doing any harm if I say some prayers while I'm having a smoke?' I liked that, but it wasn't enough to keep me in the habit, you might say."

Franklin laughed both at the wisdom of the tale and the pun at the end. He liked Robert and found his company quietly strengthening. He had picked up a depth of character somewhere, maybe from his years with the Benedictines. Franklin could easily picture him in the monastic robes. But he was just as much at home amid the din and merriment of *Rafferty's*. He was also much at ease with his two brothers, and Franklin guessed he and they communicated a lot without words.

The musical moment of the night came when a young girl got up and delivered a stunning rendition of the song *My Lagan Love* – no easy song to sing –

bringing to the surface the plaintive and exquisitely tortuous melody.

The crowd went wild. Even Robert was on his feet, applauding with gusto. Franklin too. And he took the opportunity, when everyone was looking elsewhere, to make a closer study of the blind girl, Dymphna. No question, she had him beguiled.

But Franklin had not gone entirely unnoticed, and a little while later Tommy raised the matter with him for a second time. "Frankie, you may have taken my words as casual advice. They are more than that. You know me – I'm not here to issue warnings to anybody. But you should see it as strong advice. Her family keep her well chaperoned, and for good reason. They are a very particular family; let me put it that way. They live wild. You're not over here for trouble and strife. You need to relax and have some fun. Come on, let's see if we can talk Eamonn into giving us a song this holy night."

But Franklin heard a voice saying, "Listen, would it be all right if I went up and sang? For some reason, I feel like singing. I never sing. But it's not because I can't sing. I'm just never in the mood. But you know something, I'm ready to sing now."

And the voice he heard was his own.

Eamonn went straight over to the band and whispered, and next thing the fiddler was shouting, "Now give a big hand to our friend, Fabulous Franklin, from Scotland. Come on, Franklin. Up you get. Fine fella you are!"

And up he got. He squeezed his way through the crowd and past Dymphna, looking more closely at her as he passed and wondering of the strangeness that she could not see him while he could feast on her. He conferred briefly with the band and then rolled into a Scots ballad, supposedly composed by Robert Burns. Franklin handled the doleful tune quite strongly, and gave a fine rendition to the Scots dialect in which the song is phrased, powerfully delivering lines like:

'What force or guile could ne'er subdue through many warlike ages.

Is wrought now by a coward few for hireling traitor's wages'

As the instruments began to fill in behind his voice, his confidence grew. He was even bold enough to take occasional glances at Dymphna, down to his left, and no one was more astonished than himself when the applause rang high and loud, as he concluded with the refrain which is also the title of this ballad: *Such a Parcel of Rogues in a Nation.*

His friends were delighted and impressed.

"No more bus driving for you, Frankie," declared Tommy.

But not everyone was satisfied. A large man in a bright yellow and red jersey muscled his way in. His long hair was held in a ponytail and was whitish with yellow streaks. He had a smooth, tapering chin. His eyes had a kind of gold fleck to them.

"D'ye think that was a suitable song to sing in here?" he asked.

"I do. It's a Scottish folk ballad. Robert Burns wrote the words. I'm sure you've heard of him."

"Trying to insult me? Of course I know the song. Though I couldn't recognise some of it in the skirly way you sang it. It's meant to be a war song – a call to battle."

"No. I'm sure it's not. It's a lament for the treachery of politicians, and as such, it's universal. A lot of people in this pub seemed to appreciate it. Maybe you could have listened more closely. I'm certainly not going to apologise for my Scottish accent. It's a Scottish song, for God's sake. Not every song needs to be about the IRA."

It was a good speech until that final sentence. It was a true statement, but it was not universally believed in *Rafferty's*.

"And what would somebody like you know about the IRA? Maybe that was an English song after all," suggested Yellowbeard.

"Don't be bloody ridiculous. Did you not hear the line 'We are bought and sold for English gold'?"

"You've got a bit of a smartass answer for everything. As a visitor to our country, you should show more respect."

By now this dialogue had become the focus in the pub, and many were craning over or ducking around to get a clear view of the contest. It featured as a neat break for the musicians, and it felt like an organic part of the evening. It was Robert who was first to realise the temperature was now far too high. He stood and put his hands on Yellowred's shoulders. But before he could say a calming word, the yellow jersey bounced him back down into his seat, in a move lifted from the old-time, Saturday afternoon TV wrestling. Tommy and Eamonn leapt from their seats and came to intervene, but both were long retired from the ring, and it was Franklin who got there first, hammering Yellowred on the side of the face with a clenched fist that knocked him backwards towards the bar. Yellowred came in with a short, sharp jab to the nose which brought blood. But Franklin followed through, hitting him again in the same place. He kicked the legs from under his opponent and sat bestriding his chest.

He hissed, "Now then, buddy, ever had your throat cut in *Rafferty's*?"

But already people were behind him, pulling him off by his neck and his arms. Some others did the same for the Ponytail, and the bout ended, remarkably, with a bruised cheek and a bloody nose being the only injuries. Still, it was a severe breach of the peace, and for many in the bar, a throwback to the bad, old days of pub fights every weekend. By now, two burly barmen had got round to the epicentre, and each grabbed one of the contestants and held him close until the manager arrived. Several patrons tried to provide an account of the squabble that led to it.

"Youse are both to leave these premises right now and consider yourselves barred for three months. However, I will defer this punishment if the two of youse shake hands sincerely and promise to avoid all such ructions in here for the future."

They shook hands quite solemnly, perhaps aware that they had been let off lightly. The tall man, whose name now turned out to be Big Charlie, went a step further and insisted on buying a round of drinks for Franklin and his party. This was duly accepted, and within minutes the music was resumed with one of Tommy Makem's old hits, *Brennan on the Moor*.

Tommy asked if they felt they should go elsewhere, since it was only just after eleven, and it might be wise to avoid any possibility of repercussions. Franklin looked at Tommy and thought, *For somebody who likes his Mass and his rosary, he sure does like his Saturday nights to be full-length.* He wanted to stay where they were, pointing out the weak reason that a fresh round of drinks was on its way, courtesy of their new friend and sparring-partner, Big Charlie. Robert said he was quite settled, especially now that the boxing programme was over.

Soon the crowd began to thin out a little, and Franklin noticed that there was more space beside Dymphna. He was rehearsing a line of introduction in his head and was just about to move over. But he paused. He recalled Tommy's serious remarks about the girl and added to that the fact that after the recent uproar, he had little credit left should anything else go wrong. So he sat back with his pals and enjoyed the rest of the music.

He was telling of some personal event to Robert when Robert put a hand on his arm and pointed – Big Charlie was on the rostrum and about to sing. He was applauded before he even got started.

Franklin felt something clutch at his heart when Charlie said, "I wonder if I might ask the lovely Dymphna O'Connell to join me in a little duet."

Dymphna rose immediately and was guided up to the rostrum, where Charlie helped to place her beside him and in front of Colum the banjo player. They set off in perfect timing through the age-old ballad, *Barbara Allen*, Dymphna's harmonies bringing out the yearning and sadness at the heart of the song. The applause poured across the rafters.

Robert said to Franklin, "If you had a mind to now, you could turn that recent little skirmish into Armageddon. But I hope you won't."

Robert's intuition helped Franklin to calm himself. In a moment of clarity, he saw how he was being beguiled, being drawn into a fairy fantasy such as Ireland is famed for. Franklin and Dymphna? No, it would never, ever be. Never. Yet he found himself looking for a plan to meet her, to talk with her for just a little while, convinced that this was destiny at work.

Chapter 14

It has been said that no Irishman with any pride ever used the hangover as an excuse to miss Sunday Mass. Franklin remembered being told that long ago. So he was prepared on Sunday morning to be recruited into active service; no lazing in bed or complaining of a sore head on the Sabbath. He felt quite sober, enough to remember both Dymphna and Big Charlie but, as ever, some fuzziness remained. He expected Tommy would have a plan to pray at Mass for the Yellowbeard. He was correct, although a full Irish breakfast at ten o'clock was enjoyed by all, and as the morning ticked away, Franklin began to feel hopeful. Until Tommy informed him that there was a High Mass over at Phibsborough at twelve on Sundays, and it being a majestic experience, they proposed to go over there. It was Catherine's local Church, St Peter's. They would meet the Reillys there, have a light lunch afterwards at their house, and then go along to have a game of pitch-and-putt at the local course.

Franklin noticed that none of this was presented as optional. He also detected some coldness in the vibrations from his hosts. After his bout the night before, he thought it better to play along with what was asked. Without reviewing the evidence, he felt that he was doing all right; that he had been getting on form and making a good impression.

That was not the way Eamonn and Tommy were seeing it. They saw a relative – to whom they therefore owed some hospitality – who seemed to trail trouble along with him everywhere. As men who had made a fair attempt to put their own lives in order and be of use to the community, it grieved and disappointed both to witness their younger cousin in such a ramshackle state, with no direction home, as someone once put it. It was Franklin, not Big Charlie, they intended to pray for at Mass.

"Do you enjoy going to Mass, Montgomery?" whispered Franklin from the end of the pew where he was sat next to the youngster.

"Yes, I do, although sometimes I fall asleep. Depends which priest is on. I like these sung Masses. Reminds me a bit of a – well, not a pantomime, but a show of some sort. Do you know any Latin, Uncle Franklin?"

"No. Nothing except the little I remember from my time as an altar boy. Long ago, of course. *Ad Deum qui laetificat juventutem meum.*"

"Well done, uncle! I know that bit. It's the start of the prayers at the foot of the altar. I've started doing Latin at school, but it's quite a bit different from the Church Latin. I like the Latin Mass because you can sit and listen to all the different bits. There's less bobbing up and down, standing, kneeling and sitting than there is at ordinary Masses."

Montgomery was too busy enjoying nattering to his new uncle to notice that Franklin had grasped his side as if in extreme pain, his face was contorted, a cold sweat beaded his brow. A woman in the pew in front turned round and gave them a very disapproving look. But a minute later, Montgomery tugged on Franklin's sleeve.

In a low voice, he whispered, "I like the incense, too. I love it when it's strong and cloudy. Great smell. Makes me a little dizzy, but in a good way."

A bell rang, the procession came down the centre aisle, and the choir got started on the entry antiphon. Franklin, too, was suddenly able to relax a little and not worry about which move was next. He glanced along at Catherine several times, and once he got a lovely smile. But he knew she was troubled about him.

At lunch round Reillys' table, the crowd was jolly and at ease. Even Franklin was smiling without having to think about it. As they nattered, Eamonn remarked to Montgomery that his Uncle Frank used to be a boxer before he was a bus driver. This did not have the effect Eamonn probably intended, and the silence that fell alerted Catherine to some sub-text. She tried to keep her concern low, asking whether Eamonn knew this from the history of boxing, or had he seen Franklin in a fight?

This was not the point for Franklin to add anything, but he made a mistake and said, "Yes, Catherine, he saw me in action. Only last night. In *Rafferty's*. A big, giant of a guy all in red and yellow deliberately provoked me, picked a fight with me and landed on his back. And that was it, over and done with. In fact, he bought us a round as a gesture of atonement. Is that the right word, Montgomery?"

"It sounds as if it is, Uncle Franklin. That kind of stuff happens a lot here. If the guy you socked was dressed half in yellow and half in red it was probably The Pied Piper – the Pied Piper of Dubalin." Montgomery bowed modestly at the applause which greeted this. "But is it true what Uncle Eamonn says that you were once a boxer?"

"No. It's not true. Eamonn likes a wee joke. Not a professional boxer. I have been in a few fights, but they don't count."

"No, I didn't believe you were a boxer. But I still believe you were a bus driver before you became successful. "

The table recovered some equanimity, but Catherine still needed to add, "Montgomery, fighting in a bar is not being a success. The very opposite. Dad, why do you take visitors and family like Franklin to these pubs? Was there sawdust on the floor? Do they slide the whiskey along the bar? We know these places thrive on *The Soldier's Song* and *The Bold Fenian Men*. We've had enough of that. No doubt Franklin can take care of himself. But are we never to make any progress culturally in Ireland?"

"That is a very important question indeed, Catherine. But Franklin is over to get a break from the sort of stresses and worries of his everyday life. It may well be that he's not looking for cultural interest on this visit. You've known him, after all. You could hardly be surprised that he's preferred the pubs to the museums. He is what he is. He gave us no notice of his proposed visit. Doesn't that suggest a man who just can't go on unless he gets a break from his troubles?"

Franklin, listening intently to this chat, paused to consider: 'He is what he is'. Very precise. *But what am I?* he thought. *As soon as I get some sense of who I am, I do something that completely runs against that version of myself. Just as often, I could say, 'I am what I'm not'. I stole that briefcase last month. It was empty. Crimes don't seem to register with me. Eloping with a blind girl is much more to my liking. I would concentrate everything on that. Sure to be exciting. There'd be no forgetting.*

He was jolted back into the present to see everyone looking at him. Someone must have asked him a question, and he didn't know who, or what.

"Sorry, I've been in a dream. I was thinking about that High Mass; how they've been doing that exactly like that for such a long time. It's amazing. And Catherine mentioned culture, and I was thinking of a very interesting exhibition I went to last time I was over.

It was all on that poet Yeats. I do remember being amazed at the range and variety of his poems. So, I was drifting... did somebody ask me a question? Was it you, Robert?"

"It was, Franklin. Just asking do you remember the time you and Catherine and I went to the Abbey and saw *Endgame*?"

"The people in the bins? What's his name? – Hamm? Oh, yes, I do recall that night. We had a good argument then, too, if I remember. Catherine was explaining what Beckett was after in this weird play, and I was trying to prove it was too crazy to be understood. I happened to agree with Catherine, but I was so enjoying the discussion we were having that I wanted to prolong it. That was a bit dishonest of me. Not like me at all, hahaha."

"That's right. I got a bit worried you were going to have a fight there and then in the Abbey bar. But you see what I mean? Fights do seem to follow you around. Do you fight a lot in Glasgow? The place has a reputation."

The directness of Robert's question, as well as its pointedness, took Franklin off guard. He decided to try some humour to divert all this focus on his character.

"I sometimes fight with furniture. I got into a fight a week ago with a large armchair and ended up throwing it out of the window. But that is a rare occasion. No, I'm not a fighter. I never, ever go looking for a fight."

This move was effective – there was chuckling and laughing.

Montgomery said, "I don't know what all the fuss is about. I think it's great fun to have a crazy uncle who fights with armchairs. What a laugh!"

It started to rain quite heavily, and pitch-and-putt was unanimously abandoned. Montgomery asked for permission to use the computer and was granted two hours.

Robert then had a surprising proposal. "Glasgow and Dublin have a lot in common. And in coming to Dublin, you're only exchanging one city for another similar one. Okay, they have differences, too, but the break from stress you seem to be searching for – it might be best to get out of cities for a bit. Now what I'm thinking is: I must go up and see a fella – a farmer – in the Wicklow Mountains. I'll be staying there overnight – he never lets me leave the same day. Sometimes it's been two days. Why don't you come along? You'll see a different kind of Ireland; you'll maybe meet one or two interesting people. It'll be a nice, wee change from this old smoky place– if you're staying on, that is, for a few days yet. What do you think, Tommy? Tim? Eamonn?"

All were in loud agreement, so much that even Franklin could see how they would be glad of a break from his company for a few days.

"I like the idea. I do. I've seen little of Ireland outside its main cities and a few wee towns. Maybe I'll get some exercise, which I badly need."

"Yes, indeed, Franklin. There's a little work involved, and you'll be very useful. Will you accept the minimum hourly rate for agricultural workers?"

Franklin laughed, caught up by the whole proposal. He carried some glasses into the kitchen where Catherine was clearing up.

"Did you hear that plot to send me into exile? In the mountains?" he asked.

"Franklin, it'll be a lovely little breath of fresh air for you. Literally. It's thrilling up there. Take your coat. And watch out for the leprechauns. I'm not kidding about that. Wicklow Mountains is a land of magic. We'll see you in a couple of days if the wee folk don't capture you. When do you go back to Glasgow?"

"I don't know yet."

"Franklin, can I ask: what do you do? For a living, I mean."

"That sounds like a simple question. But believe me, the answer is far from simple. I've always liked being sort of freelance, rather than at the beck and call of some employer. I know that makes me sound arrogant and special, which I'm not, but I've managed to get along that way – by being available for odd and unusual work, maybe short-term, and I've never gone very long without some way of money coming in. I'm not rich. I'm not poor."

"Maybe I shouldn't have asked. Because that's a very clever and roundabout way of avoiding the question. And I tell you, it kinda sounds like there's something you're keeping back. I used to be able to tell when that was happening, don't you remember? Well, it's your life. You were always a kind of a vagabond, it's true. But you have certainly made a big impact on my Montgomery. He is enthralled by you. I would never discourage that. He does see things that we don't, and maybe he sees things in you that others can't. Anyway, before you go, if you're not going to give me an answer, can I take a guess?"

"Nothing to stop you."

"I'll leave bus driver aside. And boxer. And I'll guess gangster."

"Oh, come on. I'm disappointed. You know I'm too good-looking to be a gangster."

"Maybe once upon a time. You're letting yourself go to seed a bit. I'm disappointed."

"You're wrong – I'm not a gangster. However, I do know some gangsters. One or two of them have done me favours in the past. For which I've had to return the favour. It's a market, like other markets, but this one does depend a lot on your personal word – you must mean what you say, or the system is in trouble."

"Well, I got to say, Franklin, trustworthiness is not your biggest asset. You do have some, but you're not strong on trust. Tim has faults, but he's a good man. I can trust him. I got lucky."

A call of "Oi! Where's that apple pie got to?" came through to the kitchen, and the discussion ended prematurely.

Tim explained to Franklin that they would both be working all week, and so in case they didn't get another chance to see him while he was over, they proposed to take him out for dinner that Sunday night, at *McGrath's Steakhouse* just off O'Connell Street. They would meet at the *Tower Bar* –now renamed *The Lunar Six* – in Henry Street, about seven thirty.

Chapter 15

They were watching some televised football from Croke Park. Tommy informed Franklin that the Rosary and Benediction service at St Dominic's at six o'clock was a lovely experience.

This time, Franklin was more firm with his host. "No thanks, Tommy. I'll just put the feet up until I go out to meet Tim and Catherine. And maybe Montgomery. I do need to build up my reserves before meeting him."

"You'll be OK there. Montgomery won't be coming. They draw quite a strict line, and there's a lovely neighbour who just adores babysitting the young fella. So you can relax. Still, if you've had enough of the Rosary for the time being, we'll give you a dispensation."

Tim and Eamonn departed at 5.40, and right on their heels was Franklin, heading downtown for a refresher before the evening session. He thought of *Lanigan's* but decided it would be a shame not to try for a little more variety. He saw a bar he had a dim memory of, called *Brannigan's*. He took a Guinness and sat at a table near where an elderly couple were sitting.

When the lady went to the toilet, the gentleman informed Franklin that he had spent thirty years building the railway. Franklin congratulated him, thinking that was the response expected. Not quite.

"Whaddya mean, well done? It nearly kilt me. I'm six feet and 2 inches: by right I should be five feet and 4 inches. That was where I started off. You know what did it? Pacing along those sleepers, day after day. They were spaced out more back then; big steps needed. They've changed all that, distance a lot shorter now. But I spent so much of my younger days stretching and stretching the legs all day. The thing was, your legs got so used to the big strides, that it kept them going, even when you were walking along the street. I put on nearly a foot in height."

Franklin felt uncertain about a response. Why did he keep finding these people?

But before he could reply, the old boy asked him, "Did you ever think of being a train driver?"

"No. Can't say I did."

"Why not? It's a fine career."

"I was following other interests. I like trains – I've travelled on many trains. But that doesn't mean I want to drive them."

"I was training to be a train driver. It was the only thing for me. I loved trains. Since I was very young. Obsessed, that was what I was. And I was looking forward to driving, when guess what? I failed the eyesight test. My distance vision was below the required standard. They felt sorry for me. Knew how I loved trains. So they offered me a job building the railways. Back then there was still a lot of lines to be laid. Thirty years I was that guy in the song, *Paddy Works on the Railway*."

Before he could break into a rendition of this song, as he no doubt intended, the lady returned.

"Pleased to meet you," she said. "I'm Margaret. This here is Sean. I won't ask what you've been talking about. Railway lines. My God, what a wasted life I've had. Nothing but bloody railways. It got so bad I had to protest, and I did – I haven't been on a train in ten years, coming up eleven. He's driven me mad, that eejit. Unfortunately, every country in the whole world now has railways. There's nowhere I can escape to."

"Sorry about that. Maybe I could buy you a drink."

"Gordon's gin and Indian Tonic for me, please. He'll take a pint of stout."

"A pint of stout now and again does you no harm. Sailors that go away and work in ships, they've always had a good ration of rum. Us railway men got nothin. They could've included the odd pint of stout at our work-break. But no."

"You see what I mean? Everything comes back to railways. Trains on the brain. Da, will ya shut up about the railways and let the gentleman get a word in. He can be a handful sometimes, especially if he overdoes his ration of stout. I call in on him as often as I can, but I have a life of my own."

By then she had removed her coat and bonnet, and Franklin saw that she was indeed a lot younger than the railwayman.

"Oh, I, eh, sorry, I'm embarrassed – at first took you for a couple."

"Oh, Jaysus, now I've heard it all. This is me father, Sean, and I'm his daughter."

"Yes, I mean, I only saw you from the back, and well, my mistake, obviously. You are looking well."

She tackled her gin with gusto, and the three of them were nattering away inconsequentially (and incomprehensibly for Franklin, a lot of the time) when they were joined by a still younger woman.

"Ah, Sinead, there you are, darlin. Sit down there beside Granda. This is my new friend, Kremlin. You timed it nice, as usual. It's my round. What'll you have?"

"Diet coke, ma. I have the car."

"Leave it and catch the Dart back over."

"I don't believe I'm hearing you telling me to take a train instead of my car."

This gave Sean a chance to re-take the reins.

"And what part of England are you from, Frank?"

"Not any part. No, I'm from Glasgow, in Scotland."

Margaret had returned with the drinks and didn't like the sound of that.

"Glasgow, eh? It's a miracle you've survived. Terrible place. Gangs. Razors: they still carry razors, they tell me. Tried to get rid of them back in the thirties, but the Billy Boys weren't having any of that. Nor the Conks, for that matter."

Granda was not finished.

"The Billy Boys controlled all east Glasgow, but right in the middle of their territory was Norman Street, a fanatically pro-Irish enclave. In the coronation of 1953, they painted all the walls in Norman Street green, white and gold and strung banners across the street. No Billy Boy dared go in there to protest."

"I'm impressed at your knowledge of Glasgow. Have you visited it much?"

"Never been," said Sean.

Nor had Margaret.

"No, me neither. I was in Edinburgh once and asked about seeing Glasgow, but I was told, in no uncertain terms, not to go there. That my Dublin accent would place me in danger. Of course, lots of Dubliners go to and from Glasgow, and they pass on stories, so we get to know quite a lot."

Sinead had been watching Franklin.

"Still, you must like it, eh? After all, you stay there."

"I don't know if I like it. I don't know why I stay there, either. I think maybe you young people are more hopeful and confident about the choices you can make, than we are. I'm only here on a short break and to see some relatives. But maybe I'll stay on a bit – I don't know."

"Must be nice to have that opportunity and be free. I suppose you're retired."

"Yes, just quite recently. Well, you know, a few months ago. Have a few things going, but nothing to stop me having a lie-in in the morning."

Margaret felt it was time to take back control.

"Lave poor Kremlin alone with your questions now. The poor man is trying to have a wee drink during his weekend break, and here we are lambasting him with interrogations."

Franklin's phone rang. He lifted it, and his rheumy eyes widened. It was Catherine asking where he was – they were to meet at seven thirty. Their table was booked for eight. Where was he?

"So sorry, Catherine. Got caught up in some conversation and lost track of time. 7.50. OK, I'll just head straight to *McGrath's* now and meet you there."

He apologised to his latest troupe of friends, and as he headed out of *Brannigan's*, he saw Sean reaching for Franklin's untouched whiskey.

They were eating their starter course in *McGrath's*, Catherine and Tim very stylishly dressed, and Franklin looking scruffy.

When they met by the door, Catherine had looked at him, and asked, "Do you still have that nice green suit you wore last time? You looked quite elegant in it."

"No. Don't have that one now. In fact, I have only one suit; a black one, for certain occasions. Couldn't see the point in having all those others that I never wore. I sold them in a batch to a guy who said he's taking a risk, even though he was a good deal fatter than me. But I never heard any more about them. I go casual nearly all the time."

"You'll find this hard to believe, Tim, but cousin Franklin here, or whatever he is, used to be my idea of a good, regular guy – and especially a guy you could trust and rely on. Now I hear of him singing loud, offensive songs, getting into a drunken brawl, setting a very bad example to our son, and now he can't even respect our invitation to a meal. Franklin, honestly, are you like this all the time now? Have you gone to the dogs, as they used to say?"

What puzzled Franklin in all this was the overtly sharp and scolding tone Catherine took. He tried to recall being with her years ago. She had always been forthright, but not to this extent. If a woman in Glasgow spoke like this to Franklin, she would be in some danger. Yet he was just not angry enough with her to feel dangerous. But even people he was fond of did not address him in these insulting terms.

Tim turned the talk into less prickly ground, and chatted for a while with Franklin about golf, an interest they shared. Franklin confessed he rarely played a full round now, but always enjoyed watching the big tournaments on television. Tim was a member over at *Portmarnock*, a classy club, and when they had sorted out some golf issues, Catherine was in a more relaxed state. On his last visit, she had only rarely taken any kind of alcohol. But she was catching up. The level of red wine in her glass did not long sink below three-quarters full. She was fully attentive when Tim mentioned the subject of work

"So you've been able to retire, Franklin? Feel OK about that? I would think it's a lot of years still to fill. OK if you've got a great pension, I suppose."

"Well, not fully retired," explained Franklin. "Just from my latest job. I mean, of course I do intend to do other things. I'm not even fifty."

"So what were you doing?"

"TEFL work. You know what that is? Teaching English as a Foreign Language. In a college in Glasgow, to European students, mostly from Italy and Spain. But there has been a lot of political stuff going on, and these days you're walking on glass – one false phrase and you're on trial for racism or sexism or God knows what. I just felt recently that my health was suffering, and I packed it in. I do have some other interests that pay for the petrol, but soon I'll have to start looking around."

Franklin was relieved but a little surprised that Tim did not respond to any of this, except for a vague nodding of the head. Maybe Franklin sensed Tim's wish to steer away from controversy at this point.

Catherine was less cautious. "Is Agnes OK with all of this?"

"What? What did you say?"

"Agnes – your wife. Isn't her name Agnes?"

Franklin had that against-the-ropes feeling he was so familiar with.

"Agnes is long gone," he replied. "Did I not tell you? Agnes disappeared a few years ago."

"What, like disappeared? You mean, literally? Or she just ran off and left you? Yes, and I wonder why, eh?"

Tim, astonished at this turn of events, set aside his passive demeanour. "Cath! Catherine, take it easy! You're going for the jugular, and this is a friendly meal, not a back-alley fight. We're in *McGrath's*. A place you love. Let's all take a deep breath."

They did, and Catherine and Franklin added a deep draught of wine to the breath. Tim's intervention paid off, and Catherine calmed down and changed to a tearful apology. All three held hands in a circle, relief on all three faces.

"Sorry, Franklin. So sorry. You know I'm always fond of you. I would never hurt you. I'm so mixed up. You seem so changed, so... I don't know how to take you. And it's got me in a right muddle."

"Thanks for that, Catherine. That's why I try to avoid getting emotional about things. It always comes back in your face. In fifteen years, we've all changed, no doubt. Except maybe your father, that lovely man. Anyway, thanks, Tim, for finding the brakes there – a big help. Why don't we bury all these problems in a lovely dessert and some more wine?"

While they waited, more relaxed, Franklin said, "Can I just add; this matter is too painful to talk about. I'm still struggling to cope with that whole business. Thinking about it makes me ill. I never talk about it. It will pass away eventually."

The discussion turned to his coming trip up into Wicklow, and he got some information about what to expect. Not a great deal, though, because neither of them seemed to have been in the mountains since they were small. At that time, the threat of being magicked away by leprechauns they took seriously. Their beliefs in the existence and ways of the little people did not seem to have vanished altogether. Franklin chuckled in surprise at what he took as childish naivete in these two cultured professionals. He asked for advice, and Catherine offered some.

"Robert is a great practical joker," she said. "He does not look a joker of any kind, but he loves playing tricks on folk. He'll have something prepared for you, I know."

"Yes, that's funny, because I thought I could see another Robert inside the Robert, if you know what I mean."

Tim had some explanation.

"That's Bob you're seeing. Bad Bob. Remembered that great film with Paul Newman as *The Life and Times of Judge Roy Bean*? One of the villains in that western was known as Bad Bob the Albino. I've read interpretations that he was a demon, or a version of a demon, and flitted from person to person and lived for centuries. So maybe Bad Bob has made a home in Robert Jordan."

"If Robert's a demon, then I'm in terrible trouble," declared Franklin.

They exchanged phone numbers, hugged, and when the taxi came, even Franklin had a tear in his eye. The night had fallen short, another opportunity gone, and only one to blame. He waved to the taxi then started to saunter home alone. Walking along Talbot Street, he remembered he had switched off his phone. He checked, and one email number caught his eye. It was Mr Patrick's. He had to stand still to read the message, dated six hours earlier.

'Disappointed no photo forthcoming and no explanation. Reparation still possible. Bro Kurt has deputed me to allocate you a task. So it will be to provide me with, not a photo, but the present address of the same person. One week from this date seems a reasonable time to allow for this assignment. Telephone number if possible, also, but full address and postcode minimum. Remember not to use open line when sending details. Bro Patrick'

What a long, dark street this Talbot Street is, Franklin thought, lost in the bottom of Palm Sunday.

Chapter 16

"Franklin! I know you've had dinner, but we've just about to have some lovely, toasted cheese, if you want to join us."

"I'll be right with you, Eamonn."

The sight of the two elderly brothers at the table with their tea and supper calmed Franklin a little, and the sigh of relief he uttered as he joined them was noticed.

"Everything OK? Have a nice meal in *McGrath's*?"

"Yes. I did. "

But his voice was flat, and he realised something would have to be explained.

"Actually, it got off to a bad start because I was late. I left here early, called in for a snifter at *Brannigan's*, and got involved chatting to a family of real Dubliners, especially the auld fella who kept telling me about his years working on the railway. Anyway, I lost track of time and got to the restaurant ten minutes late. Catherine was not pleased. And after some wine had been taken, she let me know it! But it all got sorted out, don't worry. We're still the best of pals. Tim was a very good – and fair – referee. I didn't know he was so keen on golf."

"Yes – and a pretty good amateur, too. He plays at *Portmarnock*, a tough course. But I'm glad things didn't get out of hand."

Eamonn continued in this vein for a little longer, while Tommy munched quietly on his toasted cheese.

When he was ready, he took a long draught of tea and said, "Are you ready for your trip up into the Wicklows? Take a jersey – it can be cold. How are you with animals?"

"What d'you mean, animals?"

"Sheep, goats, cattle, pigs. You'll be sure to meet some of them. That's the kind of line Robert's business is in. What about dogs? You OK with dogs?"

"Dogs and me; we get along at a distance. I've always been fine with dogs. Never had one, but a lot of people say they are good to be around."

"Franklin, me boyo, you sure have perfected the art of getting around a question. But what you haven't perfected is the art of staying out of trouble. Getting into trouble in *Rafferty's* is ordinary. But anybody who gets into trouble with Catherine and Tim Reilly must have a problem of some kind."

There was a pause. Franklin looked calmly at Tommy and sensed a possible opening if he was willing to go for it. Suddenly he felt icy cold and thought there was a door in front of him, half-open.

"Listen, friends, I wish that was the biggest problem hanging over me now. It's nearly eleven o'clock. Is it too late to tell you about a complicated matter that I don't seem able to deal with?"

They heartily insisted he go ahead and tell them, that it was never late at night, that they were here to help, and all that. He asked for a moment to gather his thoughts and get the details in place. Then he started with his work with Mr Patrick's company.

"There's a sort of company in Glasgow, all elderly men and women, that I do some occasional work for. It doesn't matter the kind of work, right now. They pay me generously. It's not full-time, just something I keep myself available for. Anyway, Patrick, who's my contact with the group, was chatting with me during a recent meeting and mentioned that he had known my mother when they were younger. And he asked did I have a photo of her that I could pass on to him – old times' sake, and all that. I said I would look, but I forgot about it. A few days later I spoke to him again, this time at a meeting of the committee to discuss a couple of slip-ups I had made. They had heard I had thrown an armchair through my window. And I had also broken an important club rule. The details don't matter. I was told I would be kept on but might have to carry out some additional task to make amends. They would get in touch with me using an agreed method. Right. So at this point, I decided I need a break, need to get away for a bit, and so I head for here. Having some adventures here, no question, but when I was walking back from

McGrath's just a while ago, the message arrived. I'll show you it."

He brought up the message on his phone and let them read the message he had already seen.

Disappointed no photo forthcoming and no explanation. Reparation still possible. Bro Kurt has deputed me to allocate you a task. So it will be to provide me with, not a photo, but the present address of the same person. One week from this date seems a reasonable time to allow for this assignment. Telephone number if possible, also, but full address and postcode minimum. Remember not to use open line when sending details. Bro Patrick

Eamonn and Tommy were two stone faces slowly returning to human form.

Eamonn said, "You haven't given us much of a picture of this club or company or whatever, and OK – maybe you can't or don't want to. But this smells fishy. Worse than fishy. You're in with some dangerous people here, Franklin. What I don't like is the cold, polite tone of it all – just like it's business, nothing personal. But you bet it is."

"Eamonn, Tommy, just let me finish the story. There's a little bit more to tell you."

"So you do some work for this organisation. You break their rules. First you're asked to bring Saint Patrick a photo of your mother. And now he wants her address. And he has given you a deadline. Right?

"I knew they kept tabs on me. They knew about that armchair business right away. And at the committee meeting one of them, a woman, asked me was I thinking of taking a little holiday. No one on earth except me knew that."

Eamonn had things to say.

"Franklin, can I just go back a minute to this matter of the chair. You say you threw it through a window. What was going on there? Sounds as if you really lost control of everything."

"I know it sounds like that when retold. But now, I was sitting relaxed in the chair, listening to the chatter. I had a few friends in, and they were talking about poltergeists. Apparently these spooks are on the rise in Scotland. Someone mentioned a séance at which a spiritualist made a table move into the air. I got a bit tired of this baloney. It was a big, old armchair I was sitting in. I lifted it up and hurled it through the front window. I said, 'That's how you make furniture move'. I did it quietly, easily and without effort. That was what was most astonishing. No one was hurt, though two wee boys going past below were lucky."

"I don't understand you there, Franklin, but OK, that's what happened. But you said you'd broken other club rules. What was that to do with?"

"Well, honestly, it's a very hard one to explain. These old folks – nearly all men – still like the company of good-looking women. By company, I mean women who are prepared to undress for them, to sit beside them, to allow them to touch gently and to look at them without any threat of being groped or anything further. Now, I have never been present at any sessions where this was going on. I'm a C-class member. The women are B-class. And the patrons are A-class. It is hard to believe, but the women themselves, from what I've been able to find out from them, confirm that it's a very pleasant and not invasive relationship. Patrick describes it as where innocence meets sensuality. Of course, they are ultra-careful about who gets in and about the privacy and confidentiality that must surround the whole business. The women are well paid. C-members like me are also well paid, on a different scale, of course. I can't be sure it is what it says it is. Anyway, last Monday, one of the women, let's call her Jeannie, was due to meet me to be primed about her interview. To save travel and time, because she lived near me, I arranged for her to come to my home. I had thought Ruth was at work, but she wasn't. She was in bed. She came in, and Jeannie's cover was exposed. She lost the head and stormed out in anger at my carelessness. This got found out right away, and I was summoned to the meeting as I've told you."

"So what you're being asked is to supply this company with your mother's address? Do you know the address, for a start?"

"It's about twelve years since I've seen my mother. We had a falling out. She's half Italian, half Irish, as you know. You're first cousins. From the way you're speaking, she's never been in touch with you, either, all this time. I could get somebody to find her, I suppose. A private eye."

"And what? Tell the private eye to pick her up and take her to Saint Patrick? Franklin, this sounds dangerous to me indeed. The whole business of looking for Carmella would be traumatic, never mind finding her. You're in a mess, and the first thing is – don't go any further in. No private eyes. No promises to Patrick. But your mother may be in danger. How do you feel about that? I mean, are you still at war with one another?"

"When I divorced Agnes, my mother said she was disowning me. She said it calmy, and she meant it."

"And who is Agnes? Your wife?"

"My ex-wife. I married her just after I was last here. It only lasted two years. I was a lot to blame, and I decided not to go down that path again. My mother may still be in Glasgow. She may even be at the same address."

Eamonn thought it was too late for Franklin just to run away.

"You must locate your mother and at least make sure she's safe. She might live in a mansion; she might not have a home. She may be living with somebody who can take care of her. She may not be alive any longer. But whatever happened between you, you can't just put your head in the sand."

Tommy took up the discussion.

"Do you have a friend who can help you in this? Someone close that you can trust?"

Franklin answered, too quickly, that there were quite a few friends he could call on. He saw right away that they didn't believe him.

"Look, maybe the Wicklow Mountains will have to wait, Franklin. This is heavy; it's serious. You should go back and see what can be done. Try to focus on getting this problem sorted and then getting yourself sorted. I'll call Robert and give him a brief summary of events without the details."

"No, you can tell Robert all about it. Why not? If you don't, he's going to wonder what's going on. Robert should be told. Listen, boys, it's touching to see you worrying about me like this. I do get into these scrapes. So far, I 've managed to get back out of them. This'll be OK. I'll handle it."

"You might call this a scrape, but to me it's something worse."

"I don't know what it is. He wanted a photo of my mother. Now he wants her address. What for? I mean, she'll be in her mid-sixties."

"A woman in her sixties can offer rewarding companionship."

"Maybe so. But Carmella? It's not the way I remember her."

The night was now in deep gloom, and nobody tried to pretend otherwise. They said their goodnights then because Tommy and Eamonn would be rising early.

Franklin promised to keep them up to date with all developments. He checked he had all their numbers in his phone.

Before going up to bed, Tommy said, "If you can get back on good terms with Saint Patrick, I'd go for that. If not, you must consider getting away from it all completely.

"You called yourself a C-member of this club. Do you know any of the other C-members?"

"I've seen a couple of people whom I took to be doing the same work as me, but I didn't meet either of them personally. It's discouraged. They're probably loners, the C-workers. That would suit the chiefs."

"Loners like you?"

"Nah, I'm not a loner. You've a short memory – did you not see me bringing the house down at *Rafferty's*?"

"Yes, indeed. You did nearly bring the house down, along with Big Charley. That doesn't mean you're not a loner."

Chapter 17

It was eight a.m., the Jordans were gone, and the house was empty. Franklin sat at the table tapping a pencil against the A4 notepad he had found. It struck him that he should not write any farewell notes until he was sure he was leaving. And that entailed booking a ferry place. That would have to be done first.

He was about to find the Stena Line number, when he heard a noise, or rather a kind of rustling, and a wheezy sound alongside it. He rose silently and was looking around for a weapon when a face appeared low down in the doorway.

"Morning, Mister Frank. Sorry to disturb you. I won't be a minute. Just going to leave food for the cat."

"Molly? It's you. Right. But wait; what cat? The boys don't have a cat."

"They don't own a cat, no, if that's your meaning. But there's a cat comes in here from time to time, and I like to leave a bit of food for it. It does often appear on a Monday, isn't that strange now?"

"I've never seen it myself, Molly, but you know best."

"Sometimes I do, that's true. Are you still off the fags, now? Don't be backsliding. You'll rue it bitterly if you light another cigarette."

"Molly! I'm OK with cigarettes. I just wish everything else was as easy."

"Yes, I could see you had problems the other night. Well, who doesn't, of course? Well, I'm away. I hope your troubles lift, and *bon courage*, if I don't see you beforetimes."

Molly shuffled away. Franklin racked his brain but found no memory of a cat in the place. Somebody in this place was crazy. *They'll be telling me next it's the cat that sings the hymns in the dead of night*, he thought.

He rang Stena but could not get a car berth until the next day, so he booked one for Tuesday three p.m. Then he smoothed out the paper and wrote,

'Dear Tommy and Eamonn,

Booked sailing for this afternoon. Will call you later in the week. Thanks for all the great hospitality and kindness. I'll be back quicker next time. Love to the Reillys, and Robert. Franklin'

He decided it would be best to pack up and get a room in a hotel for one night. That way, he wouldn't have another session worrying Tommy and Eamonn. It was Holy Week They'd be at church after work, and they'd never bump into him.

He drove towards Temple Bar. He saw several hotels and a multi-level parking centre. He took a room in a Temple Bar hotel named *Pythagoras* and went out for a stroll. He was a bit alarmed to see it was just after eleven a.m. Soon he stopped and had a burger and coke, then made a phone call.

"Hello, Buster. That you? How are you? No, I just took a wee break. Was really under pressure. Sorry about last week, by the way ... No, honest, I'll square that up. That was remiss of me...Yes... Listen, I've a favour to ask of you... Aw, don't be like that. I need a bit of help here... Yes...Yes. Listen. You knew my mother when she was around, right? I've been thinking of her. Remember that wee chat we had last Monday? You were telling me about your concerns about your mother and her intentions. I got to thinking about my own mother. Never seen her in years. Lot of bad blood, of course. A time comes, though. When you must reach out, you know? I've been wondering if I should get in touch.... Yes... Only thing is, I don't have her address. No idea where she is. Would you have any idea? No, I suppose not. No. Ah, your mother – now that's interesting. She might. She was a pal of Carmella at one time. Think you could ask her? That would be great. A big favour. Listen. I won't be back in town until tomorrow night. What about I call you on Wednesday, see if you've had any luck? What? You call me? Ok, right, sure. Buster, I mean this, it's good to talk to you. Sorry I messed up. Right. See how you get on, and we'll speak on Wednesday. Yes... Bye."

He realised he would have to call Ruth as well but decided to think over that one. Might be tricky if he arrived back too soon. Enough on his plate.

He felt himself drawn to the river, ugly old serpent that it was, with its septic colour and its creepy little currents. There was the French café, which he dodged, and there was *Lanigan's*, which he embraced. No sign of Gabriel. Franklin was relieved that he wouldn't have to explain how he messed up the great tip he'd been given, but a little sad not to have a friendly chap to talk to.

He stood drinking at the bar, thinking ahead to a possible meeting with his mother. So many questions, about the past, the present and the future. *Almost enough to overwhelm a lesser man,* he thought. *But I'll get a plan organised. First, what tone do I take if we meet?* No point in dressing it up – she could always see right through when he was lying or hiding something from her. Then, what move to suggest? That she go on the run? Very funny. How did he know whether she could still run or not? But this face to face he kept trying to set before his mind would not settle; would not be steady. The presence of Agnes kept ghosting in and taking over, and he could not see his mother clearly with Agnes in between them.

He stepped out into the sunshine and realised he had all day to spend. He turned left and strolled, his mind on distant maters, until he turned a bend and saw, a hundred yards away, an old sofa, and a person with outlandish hair sitting there. He could not resist, and approached the ancient man, who watched him steadily but offered no greeting.

"Hello, old fella. Lovely day, again. I had a wee chat with you just the other day. You don't remember?"

"I remember everything. But I think I don't know you."

"It was Saturday there. You were telling me how you liked to hear the stories of sailors returning home."

"Ah! Now I see. That was my brother you met. He's often around here. He's an annoying old pest. He frightens people, especially when he makes his howling noises. Though he's a sad case, too. I won't help him, but I won't condemn him, either. "

"What's the sad case bit?"

"From his earliest years, he wanted to go to sea – to be a sailor. On his first, and only voyage at the age of fifteen, a steel hawser snapped and tore into his legs. He has no legs now. He couldn't be a sailor. It drove him crazy, and now he sits and waits to hear the stories of sailors."

"I didn't notice he had no legs."

"You don't seem to be good at noticing the difference between things, mister. You didn't notice that I am not my brother. You're going to land in trouble. I mean, you're no youngster. By your age, you should be able to tell the differences. Otherwise, you'll never make the right decisions. And you'll be wide open to the evil one, with no defences, when he arrives to offer you that choice that will save you or destroy you."

The old man got up, his remarkable hair seeming to mingle with the sky, and came over and took Franklin's arm.

"I'd say you're just about ripe for plucking, mister. Goodbye."

He turned away and walked slowly off the quay and into an alley and was lost to sight. Franklin felt like he was made of stone.

Franklin made his way back to the hotel and took a long afternoon nap. He had some salmon fillet for dinner and tried to warn himself that he had a drive in the morning he had to be fit for, so no heavy drinking.

And so, at just after eight, he was walking through the doors of *Rafferty's* bar. It was quiet, like Monday nights all over the world. But it was not empty, and among the customers sat the blind girl, Dymphna, with another girl beside her – very short hair, tattoos and heavy makeup. Franklin stood at the bar, biting his lip and wondering. Surely, surely, here was the chance he needed to turn his life around. Surely this was meant to be. Never in his life had Franklin read any romantic fiction, or he would have known how this would end. He ordered a second vodka and was just about to down it, when the fateful decision was taken out of his hands. The tattooed girl was standing right beside him.

She whispered, "Dymphna wants to know if you'd like to join us."

"Now how would Dymphna know I was in here? Don't you mean, *you'd* like to know if I want to join you?"

"Not exactly. Dymphna's hearing is spectacular. When you called your order to the barman for a vodka and a pint of lager, Dymphna said to me, 'That's the guy I was telling you about. He sang a Scottish song on Saturday'. She recognised your voice, as she always does. Now, after all that, I hope you're not going to say no. I'm Deirdre, by the way."

"Franklin. Delighted to meet you. Lead on, Deirdre."

Franklin sat down facing the two women. The closest he had ever been to Dymphna's face, he was struck by both its contours and its strength. You could not say it was a masculine face – not at all. Yet it seemed to have absorbed some attractive, masculine features without losing any feminine beauty – a face everyone might worship. And yet the eyes were closed, and the ethereal quality this imparted only raised the face to a higher realm of mystique.

Deirdre was evidently accustomed to this situation, and she sat watching Franklin watching, with a little smile on her lips.

Franklin opened with the observation that a lot of people liked drinking on a Monday night because it was a lot quieter, and because you could get served more quickly. Deirdre reminded him that this was Holy Week, from Palm Sunday to Easter Sunday, and that it was a long Irish tradition to stay off alcohol that week. She had heard of a time when the pubs were closed all that week. Many thought this was the despotic power of the Catholic Church over the people. But she had also heard that the pubs closed then, because there was no point in them being open and empty. Empty because the Irish chose to keep Holy Week sacred like this. They were a holy people, the Irish, and didn't need to be forced to be holy.

Dymphna claimed to remember a time, not long ago, that was still much stricter than the present. "The priests are on the way out. That's for sure. But we don't know yet who's going to move in and replace them. Might be worse. Sorry, Franklin, but are you a Catholic? All this'll be very boring conversation if you're not. And being Scottish, well, you know…"

"I'm a Catholic, so you can relax. Not a very good Catholic, mind you. I always like being in a church, but I don't go often. Too lazy. You say the priests are on the way out. Maybe so, especially after all the ructions here with the child abuse. But the Church proceeds at a different pace, somehow. A big eruption of hatred or protest or scandal comes along, and everybody talks about it. But when the dust settles, there's the Church, moving, ever so slowly, towards – well, whatever its destination is."

"Franklin, I'm impressed. Not only are you a Catholic, and with a few simple improvements you could be a fine-looking man, but you're also a tremenjous speaker. I love the way you pronounce 'errrruption'.

They were silent for a bit, apart from a little private whispering between the two women. Franklin felt uncomfortable looking at Dymphna, having an irrational feeling that she might be watching him somehow. He wondered about her.

Soon he decided to ask, "Is Deirdre a Catholic name, then?"

She answered with a groan. "No, it isn't. But I'm glad at least you didn't say what everybody here says when I tell my name. They say, 'Ah! Deirdre of the Sorrows'. This Deirdre is some creature from Irish mythology, and I do wish she'd stayed mythological."

They all laughed.

Franklin asked, "And what about Dymphna? Not a name I've ever heard. Is it from the myths?"

"No, indeed it is not. Saint Dymphna is a Christian of the early church. When her mother died, her father lost his mind and started lusting after his daughter. She eventually escaped to Belgium but was caught and brought back. When she still wouldn't submit to her crazy father, he cut off her head. She's the patron saint of the insane. So, incredibly pleased to know you, Mr Franklin. Can I help you with your mental health?"

More laughter.

Franklin added, "I'd like to meet somebody who could."

The conversation was getting more and more relaxed and took a surprising turn when Dymphna said, "You know, although I cover myself up, of course, I have a fine body beneath these clothes. I do like my fun. If I was not blind, I would insist on being called 'Dymphna the Nympho'."

Franklin spluttered into his pint, his conventional preconceptions of blind women shattered in one brief remark. He felt the stirrings of curiosity and desire, and a weaker part of him tried to signal the dangers in these feelings. Franklin was no one's fool. He was everyone's fool.

Deirdre may or may not have been joking when she insisted, "Listen, Franklin, I'm here to keep her under control. Not to guide her to the toilet or onto the bus. I'm here to make sure she keeps men at a distance. Isn't that so, Dymph?"

"Nobody can keep me back when me blood is up, least of all, 'Deirdre of the Sorrows'!"

The talk went on in this style of banter for a while before turning more serious.

Franklin led the way. "Dymphna, I hope you don't mind this question. I mean no harm, but I do not know any blind people. So, isn't it a bit dangerous for a blind person to be drinking? Alcohol, I mean?"

"It's very dangerous, Frank. We are cautioned against it all the time by our carers and doctors. I like red wine. I come to this pub a lot because there's always good company. If I'm on my own, I drink diet coke. No problem. If someone is with me to see me home, I have some red wine. Deirdre here is my gateway to the... I nearly said gateway to the graveyard – to the grape! She always sees me home safe, and that's after she's had a few herself. She never tells me how many. Then often she'll just stay over at my place. I don't keep wine in the house, because I'm too fond of it, and even I can see how it would be dangerous without my sight."

"So you've no one living with you?"

"Ah, now, Frankie boy, do I detect a bit of detective work going on? Sure you'll be asking next what time do I go to bed? I've told you enough about me. What about you?"

"Oh, I'm just a bit of a rambler, over here for a break from business for a few days. Saying with some relatives over by the North Strand. Older fellas, quite religious, so this Holy Week they've been trying to convert me from my sinful ways. I'm due to drive back up to the ferry tomorrow, as some business matters require attention. But how lovely it's been meeting you two, with your exotic names and your love of life."

"Now, now – slow down, Frankie. Not so fast – the ferry's not until tomorrow. C'mon, tell us young innocents what life is like in the UK."

They were now sitting in a row.

Dymphna suggested, "Come and sit facing us, so that I can hear you, and Deirdre can see you."

"Ok, but first let me refill your glasses. Same again? Red merlot?"

When he returned with the drinks, Deirdre told him they had been doing some guessing at his occupation. Dymphna said she thought maybe a street-sweeper or a gangster. Franklin could not tell how far she was serious. Deirdre guessed at a bin-lorry driver or a parking attendant. Both kept their faces straight. Franklin could not know if they were joking and felt somewhat riled. Were they making a fool of him?

He was in this doubtful frame of mind when Dymphna called out, "Well? Come on, were either of us right?"

"Absolutely not. Wide of the mark. I'm not working just now, for health reasons. But until quite recently, I was in the music business."

"Oh, yes, you sang the other night. You were very good."

"Yes. I have a bit of a voice when I'm in the mood. But no, that's not where I was at. I was a music producer. Dealt with quite several familiar names."

"Really? We were totally wrong? Who did you produce for? Would we know them? And don't say Beyonce."

"Beyonce? Who's she? Ha-ha – no, not Beyonce. I was working quite a bit in the European market, especially Italy and Spain. You know Giorgio Bambino, the saxophone player from Milan? He was in my stable. Great talent. Walk into any jazz band. Then there was a Spanish chap, Suarez Rodriguez, one of the greatest exponents of the flamenco style. Had two successful CDs with me."

"He had two second names?"

"Bit full of himself, yes. I was glad when he moved over to Warner Brothers."

"And what music do you like to listen to, Frank?"

"Oh, Rod Stewart, Elton John, Van Morrison…"

"Van Morrison! But you're a Catholic, Frankie. Somebody once called Van Morrison, 'Ian Paisley with a guitar'."

"I didn't know Ian Paisley played the guitar."

Under the table, Dymphna kicked Deirdre's foot.

When Franklin headed for the bathroom, Deirdre leaned into Dymphna and said, "He's full of crap! He's a lying bastard! And he's a moron. But he's no match for us. He'd be easy pickings. Should we go for it?"

Dymphna advised caution. "We need to know more. Who he's with?"

"D'ya think he's just out for some fanny?"

"Maybe. Mmm… it's over a week since I had a cock."

"Yes. You practically told him you were a nympho. Behave yourself. You've always got Harold."

"Yes. Harold and his machine. No, we'll call this one off."

When Franklin returned from the bathroom with several proposals in his head, he was taken aback to see that the girls had both almost finished their wine and were preparing to leave.

"Going already?"

"It is Holy Week, Franklin. There's a meditation centre in Marlborough Street that has a late Mass for girls and women, to give them special strengths in this world of temptation."

Deirdre said this so earnestly that Franklin was taken in and surrendered right away. So much that Dymphna now wondered if she had been too cautious. Still, she always had Harold.

Each girl gave Franklin a chaste peck on each cheek and called their farewells as they headed for the door.

Franklin stood watching them go, thinking, *Hell! That was a surprise. If I didn't know better, I'd think I was losing my touch.*

He headed back to the *Pythagoras,* as if he'd only been out for a box of matches.

"Hello, Ruth. It's me, Franklin. How are you doing? Got things organised, I hope. Listen. I'll be home tonight; probably late. I know I said the weekend, but things have come up and I must be back. Oh? You are? Staying with Betsy, yes, I said that would be a good idea. Just for the time being. Well, that makes it easier. I must thank you. I mean, if we had to spend another forty-eight hours together, wouldn't be the end of the world, would it? After all, I'm not contagious. What? Whaddya mean, I'm infectious? OK, OK. You left the key. Right. I'll, eh, mebbe give you a call when – now,

now, easy does it. Ok – be like that. Listen – one more thing; how'd you and Betsy like a little holiday in Babylon? Hey, hey, go easy! Have it your way, as usual. Bye. Did you leave the key?"

That had been on the Tuesday afternoon, as the ferry was docking at Stranraer. Now here he was, turning into his street. He felt strangely nervous, as if he'd done something bad and would soon be found out. The flat had been thoroughly cleaned by Ruth, and the fresh smell in the air almost made Franklin feel grateful to her. But then he remembered how she had tired of him; she had given him ultimatums; she had left him. A new beginning lay ahead. Not immediately ahead, for there were several pressing matters outstanding. Tomorrow he would start to put things in order, take a full inventory of his life and begin anew.

When he sat down on the remaining armchair, he suddenly knew how tired the tension was making him. He took a shower, ate some cereal with milk and went to bed. The Dublin holiday was over. His head was like a bees' hive.

PART THREE

Chapter 18

As Patrick wiped off the excess shaving foam from his face, he looked in the mirror. Every day of his life, since the age of sixteen, he had shaved. Spells of illness were the only exception. He considered this simple, mundane process somehow to represent the constancy of his character and a reminder always to be humble throughout his times of happiness and success, since the good Lord had arranged for Patrick to be the beneficiary of a very rich woman's death.

At 7.55, he was in the downstairs chapel, ready for Mass at eight. Nine or ten regulars were also present. But not Bart, he noticed. After Mass, he checked his diary to see what was in store for that Wednesday: six items on the agenda, the most important being the induction of a novice B member to the Society. There was also a meeting with a leader of the local Sikh community, to discuss an exciting business matter. Then a few other items. It could take all day.

So he was in a thoughtful mood when he arrived at 8.55 at the refectory for breakfast. Kurt and Marilyn were there ahead of him. Brother Larry, who had not attended Mass, still managed to be late. But one of his legs had never recovered from a bad injury years before, and no one liked to criticize his frequent lateness.

At meals, it was the custom to keep the conversation light and casual, until Kurt, being business secretary, introduced the first matter of serious discussion.

"When we meet with Chandeep and his friends later, it would be a good idea if at least one of us showed a little knowledge of the Sikhs and their religion. Just enough to put them at ease – let them see that we have respect for their beliefs and customs."

"I know a little about them," Marilyn said. "Let me do the putting-at-ease bit. I'm good at that. And let's keep it at that. It would look too obvious if we all start throwing in remarks and observations about the Sikhs. I agree respect is important. I'll see to it."

Patrick agreed that caution was always their byword. He hated to use the word 'secrecy' but he knew, as others did, that was what he meant.

For eight years, Patrick had been the president of a secret society. But of course, they needed good business contacts to survive and prosper, and the Sikh interest promised a lot.

He suggested, "We play it carefully, and make decisions as we come to them. I'm wondering, do you think it a good idea to take them on a little stroll through the tombs?"

"Yes, that would be educational, all right. But it might upset them – they might take it wrong and think we were drawing attention to human mortality. They might wonder why. It could spoil things."

"I think you're right," answered Patrick immediately, and Marilyn noticed that these two senior members seemed to have forgotten that Larry was part of the company. Larry was not always mentally present, but Marilyn thought that the senior two should be showing him a little more respect.

Larry, however, showed no interest at all in the protocols for the visit of the Sikh Chandeep. Then surprisingly, he did comment at the end, "We should all be assured that no question of membership arises from this cultural visit. We will all recall our sworn commitment to the purity of our project. Any queries about memberships if they arise, of course, should be politely side-lined."

Long before ten a.m., they had dispersed to their various apartments. A quiet knock on Patrick's door, and Larry glided in like a bat when it moves, slowly falling and rising.

"I heard a voice from the tombs."

"You did. And rightly. I have had successive dreams that bode ill to The Levels. Although they have been my responsibility, nobody knows the locations better than you do. As you know, we agreed early on that it was the best policy that I am kept out of the detailed local information. That was put in the hands of a few trusted members. And one of them was you, Larry."

"Would you have me arrange for a lair to be made available?"

"Maybe two at the most. Will you need some help?"

"Probably. We'll see. I'm not dead yet. When do I get any details?"

"That depends. On the return of a prodigal son."

Larry appeared to leave by the window rather than the door. Patrick rubbed his eyes, and decided he was imagining things. But then he remembered that Larry was already dammed: he had not got his hands dirty, but he had supervised the intrusions into many graves. He had access to, and powers within, the tombs of The Levels, unlike Patrick, whose authority lay elsewhere in the organisation.

From his safe, Patrick took out a photo album and opened it on his desk. He flicked through a few pages and stopped at the snapshot from the early '90s of a woman in her prime, smiling confidently and proud of the effect she knew she was having. Patrick sighed, and his eyes grew moist. How different it all might have been. Yet, how the goddess fate had taken him and thrown him around like a toy, feeding him titbits of exhilaration, terror, ecstasy and despair. And at the end of it, a lasting loneliness that need never have been, if a few different steps had been taken.

The photo was of Carmella Gaddarini and showed her leaning forward, with her forearms resting on a low, overhanging tree branch, in some park. Siren and

Madonna, she had easily ensnared Johnny, though nobody understood why. Patrick continued to take out this photo and study it, though the action only brought sadness and melancholy, and occasionally, some guilt.

One day in 1988, a friend pointed out to Patrick that the number seven bus went from the stop outside his house to his office in the city. He could avoid all the stress of driving a car and the hassle of parking, by travelling by bus. So he did, and over the next year he got to know the regular drivers on the seven route. One was friendly and helpful and a merry sort of guy, whom Patrick took to like a dear friend. No doubt they would have stayed as friends had Johnny not been a little boastful.

On one occasion, when they were waiting at the city terminus, he introduced himself as Johnny Gaddarini and gabbled away about his wife and son and how marvellous they were. He proudly showed Patrick a photo of his wife, Carmella, and another of his son, Franklin. The photo of Carmella was a copy of the one Patrick now had. Patrick, struck by a bolt of yearning, knew he had to lure her away from Johnny. He was cunning enough to know this would never happen overnight, so he spent some time meditating on how his new future could be created. He did not make his move for several months, building up a dossier on the Gaddarinis with great patience. He was only forty-one, after all. He discovered that whenever his bus shifts allowed, Johnny had been attending Sunday Mass at the

Good Shepherd church, but his wife had fallen out with one of the priests, and for the sake of peace, they would now be attending St Michael's.

"That's a good idea, Johnny," said the serpentine Patrick, without dropping a stitch, "That's my parish. That's where I go. I like the ten o'clock Mass there. And the priests are very kind. It'll be great to see you there."

They met in the month of June, and Patrick had a hard job not showing too much excitement. Carmella was lovely beyond speech. And conveniently, young Franklin, paying no attention whatsoever to this stranger, was pestering his dad with questions about careers and professions and bonuses.

To Patrick's great surprise, Carmella told him, "Yes – I've seen you before, a few times. On the bus. Sometimes I travel on Johnny's bus into town. I've seen you watching him. Are you thinking of taking him away from me?"

For a giddy moment, Patrick heard the 'him' and 'me' the wrong way round. When he quickly realised his mistake, he replied, "Only to the bus depot and back."

Over the next month, they did become closer. A summer fete, held by the Church in July, gave Patrick a good chance to make progress, and the snake in the grass got closer to its prey.

Over some weak punch, an exasperated Johnny said, "*Dio mio*, Carmella – his name is Patrick, not Partick. Partick is a place in Glasgow where the 18 bus goes. He is Patrick, like the great Saint Patrick of Ireland, the one who drove all the snakes offa that island for evermore. Please, *bella mia*, get our friend's name right. Don't call him Partick."

Patrick read her smile to mean she knew what she was doing. She was just being a little impish; she was sending Patrick a sign of her affection.

And yet, over the rest of that year, Patrick never once saw her on the 7 bus. Every day he hoped, and the hope was dashed. That they would unite in the future, he had no doubt, but she was not making it easy for that dream of his to come true.

For the parish dance at Christmas, Patrick came along with an old friend who was visiting her sister for Christmas. The sister came too, along with her whiskery husband, and the four of them crammed around the same table as the three Gaddarinis. The mood was high and wild, and as the evening progressed, people lost some restraint, and thus Patrick had a chance to talk to Carmella.

He surprised her. "Carmella, I've noticed what a sharp, young fella that Franklin is. Has he started secondary school yet?"

"He started in St Andrew's in August. I don't think he likes it there. He was happier in primary. But his main friends went elsewhere. Two to St Aloysius. But of course, for that you need money. Johnny drives a bus, not a limo."

"I hope I'm not intruding, but I have noticed that you are strong practising Catholics. Have you ever thought that Franklin might have a vocation to the priesthood? I think he might make a very good priest."

"Well, excuse me, Patrick, but there are priests and there are beasts, and sometimes I cannot tell the difference."

"There may be some truth in that. But I've always thought Scottish priests were the salt of the earth."

"Yes, well, maybe they belong with the salt."

"Yes, but hear me out, Carmella. To train for the priesthood, a boy goes to a senior seminary for six years. But there are also some junior seminaries where younger boys go to get them ready earlier for their great work. And at the same time, they get an excellent secondary education. They stay in the seminary, they study there, they have the best of teachers and as much individual tuition as each needs. At the end, they have a fine certificate of Highers. The plan is that they will then go on to the senior seminary. But it's a choice. And by then, many boys, now near the end of their teenage years, have started to have second thoughts about the priesthood as a career. So they leave and return home. With an excellent school-leaving certificate. So, if you want to give a Franklin a great opening that leaves him free to choose and provides him with a top-class education, you should consider my words."

", I already know some of that. But I notice you did not mention money."

"Well, my dear Carmella, it's not for me to pry into your circumstances, but the fees involved in this project are not a concern. You discuss the whole matter with some priests and bishops, maybe, and they suggest a fair premium for you to pay. Sometimes it is zero. Yes, honestly. It's one of the great bargains of our times, and you also save on food, accommodation and all the other expenses a young teenager demands."

"I'll talk to Johnnie about it. And to Franklin, of course. They are very close. I cannot imagine that either would want to live in a different place from the other. Certainly, Franklin was an altar boy for a while, but I think he was relieved to pass through that phase."

"Yes, of course. There's no pressure. It's just a friendly idea. And if you like, I know one or two priests personally, and I could get one to come over for a chat with the three of you."

"Hell, Patrick, not so fast! Two dances, and you've almost split my family apart!"

She laughed, and so did he, but it was not a laugh shared.

A week later, he told the parish priest, "There's a quite promising young man in your parish who may have a vocation. Could you go and pay him a visit sometime? His name is Franklin, and the family name is Gaddarini."

"I know them. They've been coming here for a few months. I'll bear in mind what you say."

Patrick retreated for a while, even avoiding the seven bus, hoping to hear, before the end of August, that young Franklin was being moved out of the way of his great quest for Carmella.

Able to wait no longer, on the first Sunday of September, he returned to Sunday Mass. At the end of Mass, the three of them were waiting for him at the porch. Johnny was very pleased.

"Patrick! I am glad to see you. Have you been ill? We were worried, were we not, Carmella?"

"I was not worried. Patrick is a very healthy, fit man. He just has some crazy ideas. I think it is bad for him to be alone. Patrick, you should find a wife, a lover – somebody to take care of you. Mental illness is not understood. I have some nice women friends who would be very glad to meet you. We can talk another time. But yes, it is good to see you."

Johnny hushed her from talking too much, and said, "Well, we had a surprise visit from Father Sullivan. We are new in the parish. So he visits. He asks Franklin what he would like to do after school. Franklin said, maybe an undertaker. I never know when that boy is kidding."

Franklin, standing by, listened to this without comment, even without interest.

His mother took up the narrative. "The priest told us about the life a priest leads; what he does; why it's a good job. When he finished, he asked if Franklin have any questions. Franklin ask, 'How much is the pay?'

The priest explain, 'It is not a job for much money, but you always have the price of a packet of cigarettes'. Franklin just stared at him. 'Cigarettes?' he said. 'There are no bonuses?' So you can see why afterwards the priest say to us 'An undertaker is a very important line of work'. And leaves."

Patrick went back on the bus and back to the drawing board. Maybe he'd misjudged. Franklin was a very dissociated youngster – he would not be in the way. Johnny, of course, was the boulder in the road. But Patrick now knew every part of the number seven bus route, and exactly how long it took between stops. He always knew where Johnny would be. Unbelievably, he had not given any thought to the possibility that Carmella might turn a double shotgun on him if he made any advances. She was fiery. She was strong. He thought again of her strange remarks about his mental health and how he should find a woman for himself. That was a good one! The central plan was to be alone with her for a few hours. He never doubted that after such a meeting, she would start to belong to him. The bus driver was a lovely chap – Patrick really liked him – but what future could he offer?

Chapter 19

During the last two weeks in August, there was no Johnny on number seven. Patrick did not know whether to be excited or worried. He had not been to Mass for a few weeks. They might have left, moved, disappeared – he heard his heart beating louder. He decided he was worried, not excited. He would have to make some investigations.

Not needed. When he arrived at St Andrew's on Sundays, it was Gaddarinis everywhere. Even Franklin ran up to him and said "Hello, Paddy," which was cheeky, but Patrick was so full of relief, he just laughed. His father was nearly as bubbly with enthusiasm.

"Guess what, Patrick. I've got a different job. Well, still driving a bus, but not the same. It's a touring bus. It goes to places all over the country – England, too. And I get a uniform. I start tomorrow, with a trial run. Isn't that exciting?"

Patrick wondered who the patron saint of buses was, so that he could offer a special prayer. Then he noticed Carmella, who had not said a word, nor shown any sign of joy or any other emotion, except maybe watchfulness. For she was watching his face, and something in his soul dived for cover, aware that his plan was known, his inner evil intentions seen by her.

He was glad to escape her mind-reading by Franklin distracting him and telling him, "Dad says I can help work out the different bonuses he'll get for different tours. We'll have more money every week, not just every now and again."

Father Sullivan had reported back to him. "I don't think there's a priest there. In fact, I think there may be something very different. But it's always worth a try, so thanks, Patrick."

"Yes, of course. Did you manage to find their house, by the way?

"Yes, I had already got a note of it from Carmella – 19 Trojan Avenue. Nice place."

So now Patrick's strategy was advancing. He guessed that their first meeting could be quite short; an hour or so. There would surely be times when Franklin was out at some activity and not forever sitting working out bonuses.

When he had started at a boxing club on Friday evenings and Johnny was taking a busload to the Lake District from Friday morning till Sunday night, Patrick knew the moment had arrived. He had paved the way by talking to Carmella about a lovely book of Italian recipes he had. She had shown an interest, and he promised to bring it over to her. He would simply drop by with the book on Friday evening, and the magic would begin.

The magic never got started. The bottle of wine Patrick also brought was a bad idea and too much of a giveaway. Carmella received him gracefully. No one else was at home. She gave him some coffee, ignored the wine, but looked at some of the recipes, chatting lightly all the while. Patrick tried to turn the conversation to Johnny, but he stumbled badly, and when he asked when Johnny would be back, it came out coated in conspiracy. Carmella smiled at him openly, and never put a foot wrong.

When they stood up, she came near and said, "That's a lovely jacket you're wearing," and she slid her fingers behind the lapels and slowly drew them down. "I must see if Johnny would like one. He's so good, you know. Never spends any money on himself."

And that was that. Patrick was on the pavement in utter defeat, his hopes in pieces.

In early November, he was surprised one morning when he got on the seven bus to find Johnny back as driver. Johnny gave him a smile but looked depressed. When Patrick asked how he was, he just gave a shake of the head. Patrick, knowing this shift would end for Johnny at 1.20, made a point of being at the depot at that time. His office was not far away, and it could easily be seen as a coincidence that he bumped into Johnny. Which he did, and he fussed around him and hoped all was well.

"The tours stop for the season. I was one of the last in, so I got paid off. Luckily, the council got me back with CityBus, so here I am, once again at the bottom of the snake. You know what I mean, Patrick? Carmella is icy, and Franklin is not talking to me. Is not my fault. But they get used to things, and then these things disappear, and they get very annoyed. But I think it's only for a time. They will get used to how we were. And we were happy enough."

"Are you on the phone, Johnny? Would you like to give me your number? Because I may be able to help you. I won't say anything more here – I would need to check on a few things. But if you're available for a little extra work, very quiet, rather private, then your income could go way back up. Give me your number, and I'll phone you later in the week. Meantime, please do not mention this to anyone, even family. It's a quiet business, and I'm still not certain I can get the work for you. So—" He closed his lips and ran a finger along them, in true gangster fashion.

"Cheers, Johnny! Drink up," said Patrick to Johnny in a snug seat in *Springfield Tavern*, a dive on the other side of the tracks from where Patrick lived, but quite convenient for Johnny. "Relax, Johnny. I have some good news. If you're interested."

"What is the news?" asked Johnny.

"There's a science organisation I know about – in fact, that I'm part of – and it has lots of different jobs; some very difficult mentally; very scientific. Others are to do with running the whole machine smoothly. Others see to all the paperwork. Then others see that everybody is paid, quicky and correctly. Then there are some you could call suppliers. Their job also is hard but in a different way. It is manual work, and it calls for physical strength. In your case, it would mean doing some digging. Looking at you that should be easy. Am I right?"

"I'm strong enough to dig, yes."

"The other important thing is, it's digging in the dark. There are no lanterns, no torches. So how good is your eyesight? I mean, is there a risk you might cut off your foot with a spade?"

Johnny laughed and then saw that Patrick seemed to mean this literally. He frowned and wondered for the first time whether he should say, 'No' there and then. Before he could decide, Patrick was off again, smiling and enthusiastic.

"Right. We'll say OK to that one as well. But the digging must be as fast as humanly possible. And it must be neat and tidy and the place left in the same condition as when you arrive. You'll work with a small team, one of whom will be in total control, and you will follow his instructions without any question. Digging can get a digger dirty, of course, so when the work is finished, you will be able to get a shower and remove all traces. Then you go home and say nothing to anyone. Then you get paid. Probably by me. Now, how does that sound so far?"

"First of all, you know I drive a bus. All day, sometimes. When is this work of yours to be done?"

"At night. Always at night."

"Sometimes I am on the five thirty start in the morning."

"I know. I will never sign you in for work when you are on shifts like that. I will make sure it's when you have a late start – what they call a backshift."

"Backshift – yes, exactly. But wait. You say to tell no one. But what will Carmella say if I go out during the night?"

"Tell her you met a pal who goes night fishing. It's a well-known fact that you can catch wonderful trout at night. I know it sounds crazy. But she will believe it. You will get for the first job £300. You do not tell her you get that amount, because you would need to catch all the trout in the river. You keep some for yourself, she gets a nice sum of cash, and Franklin gets a nice, little 'bonus'. She will soon stop asking questions. I will make sure your first wage is paid very quickly."

"And when is this first job?"

"Tomorrow night."

Larry reported back that for his first attempt, Johnny had done quite well. No problem with his energy or staying power. He asked no questions and kept his focus entirely on the task, filling in afterwards with speed and strength and then exiting as per instructions. They all washed in the usual steam house, and Johnny was home around two a.m.

"Still, you don't sound completely satisfied," Patrick observed. "You got some reservation?"

"It's clear he doesn't like the work. You can tell his conscience is bothering him. He couldn't get away quick enough."

"For God's sake, Larry, it was his first time. I know Johnny. He'll do OK. He's a good man."

"That's just what worries me. Good men doing this work is the last thing we need."

Johnny did not enjoy his weekend. He had no shifts and usually would have been full of gusto for places to go to or chores to catch up on. Saturday he was low and listless, sitting in front of the television much more than he ever did. He told Carmella that he must have caught a bug at the trout fishing. He was very shivery. He drank three beers instead of his usual one. Early on Sunday, the phone rang.

"Hello, Johnny. How are you? You did well. I got a good report on you. You okay? What's up?"

"Mr Patrick, I've been kinda sick over yesterday. My stomach has been bad. It's still bad. I don't know if I'm the right man for this. I'm just getting ready to go to Mass."

"Yes, me too. That's good – I'll see you there. Don't worry – it's just nerves. Everybody gets them, especially the first time. You'll be OK, Johnny."

Patrick, for the first time, was pleased to see that Carmella wasn't at Mass. Not feeling too good, said Johnny. After they stood and chatted as always, and when Franklin told his dad he was going to make his own way home, they waved him off with a few jokes.

Then Patrick took an envelope out of his inside pocket and placed it carefully in the folds of the Catholic Observer that he had just bought. He handed the paper over to Johnny. "Great little paper that. You know you're getting the truth there." He said this rather loudly, and one or two people smiled at such rare and simple faith. To Johnny he whispered, "First wage. Be careful what you do with it. Call you in a week or two."

Johnny waited till he had walked a quarter mile and turned into a tree-lined avenue behind his own street. There he looked into the envelope, riffed through the notes and put it in his jacket. He placed the Catholic Observer in the nearest waste bin.

The pattern that followed was anticipated by Patrick. The following Sunday, Carmella appeared at Mass in a lovely new dress, walking arm in arm with Johnny. Franklin told Patrick, with some pride and uncharacteristic friendliness about his new video game.

Two weeks later, the next job was due, and Johnny, with his family now loving and together again, was saying he would rather not go on any more fishing expeditions. Patrick was calm and understanding during their discussion, but he was patient and soothing, and Johnny was no match for his wiles.

Over the following months, Johnny assisted with five digging jobs. There was no outward sign that he was boasting about his new income, nor spending it wildly, which was one aspect that worried Patrick a little. Johnny would now say little on the phone, turn up and do the job and collect his fee. He had stopped coming to Mass on Sundays – another concern – though this was a more tolerable one for Patrick, since it gave him a little more tie with Carmella, whom he continued to worship in his heart. She was pleasant and chatty with him, smiled a lot, but gave no encouragement to his amorous ambitions.

Then in March, when the hard ground of winter was at last beginning to soften, Johnny disappeared. On his last job, he had been flustered and nervous, his work had been below the usual standard, he had been too slow, and he had got into a shouting match with Larry.

Patrick's phone rang, and the caller sounded confused for a moment. He recognised her – it was Carmella. At first, it was clear she did not know who she was talking to. Then there was a pause.

"It's Patrick? It's you – this number is you? How does Johnny have your number? Your number is in the little book. I know the other numbers. There are not many. I did not know this one, so I called it. It's you! Why did I not think of that?

"Carmella – is something wrong? You sound confused. Can I do something to help you?"

"Maybe you are asking the wrong question, Patrick, or maybe you are asking the wrong person. Johnny has not come home. What a coincidence that the first number I try in his book is you."

And she hung up.

Chapter 20

Patrick placed the photo back in the album and locked it away.

All these years, he thought. *And the ghosts have never left me. I'm not surprised. What choice have they?*

Marilyn had come in and heard him talking quietly but was unfussed.

"Ah, dearest Marilyn. Do you look forward to being a ghost?"

"I do – quite heartily, really. But not yet. When my teeth start to fall out, I'll give that matter full attention. Now, the Tombs situation is this…"

Not far away, Franklin was drinking coffee and frying some bacon for a roll. Before the morning was over, there was a text message from Buster. 'Got something useful to you. *Café Marino* one o'clock. If not, phone me soon as.'

"Buster the bastard," said Franklin with his usual affection he kept for his friends.

The Marino was crowded, a very popular lunch spot, and Franklin just saw Buster's large, white arm waving away near a window. Franklin used the familiar smell of Buster's full Scottish Breakfast to guide him through to the table where he sat.

"Well, well – so you didn't get a tan. What kind of holiday is that?"

Franklin permitted him to jest for a minute. Feeling an excitement in his stomach, he asked Buster what he had found.

"Well, right away I must tell you, not the address. My ma has not been in touch with her since she moved from Bearsden, and that's at least two years. Where she went to, nobody knows. I mean, nobody that I know, knows. However, there's hope. My ma still has her mobile phone number. Here – I've written it down for you: 07805 662214. Best I can do. OK?"

"Buster, where would I be without you? I'm sorry again about that episode last week. I wasn't myself. In fact, I can tell you, now that I've had a wee break and a chance to think quietly, I have several things to see about, things I must straighten out. This may well be a start for that. I know you must get back to the shop. I'm going to be busy, too. I'll keep you right up to date. Here, for your trouble."

He passed a flat, crisp fifty pound note across the formica to Buster, whose mouth would have fallen open if he had not been busy consuming his final sausage.

Franklin strolled down to Richard's Pond, went down the steps to the walkway and stopped to sit on a green bench. He looked at the phone number, and his insides started to tighten. He felt it was certain that his life might take a huge change, and he just could not tell if it would be for better or worse. He feared that the capital sin of sloth, which ran rampant in him, was soon to be moved aside in favour of something more powerful. Sloth is, by its nature, slow to move aside.

And there was Franklin that evening in the *Ewe and Lamb* again, drinking with Dastardly Dave and his friend, Calypso. He had still not used that phone number he had been so anxious about. He was the same old Franklin, as his account of the morning demonstrated.

"Lovely Spring, late morning, I'm sitting on a bench at Richard's Pond – you know, that wee, quiet nature reserve down by the hospital. Drinking a can of diet coke. I see a white-haired, little old lady, towing her granddaughter along, both carrying bags of crumbs. She comes right up close and quacks, 'Do you know where the ducklings are?' I paused and said, 'Sorry. I don't.' She continued, 'There are eight or ten of them.' And looked at me. I explained, 'I haven't been down at the pond for a few days.' But this was not good enough for little Mother Earth. 'They've been here for at least a week,' she said accusingly. I saw some small birds between the two swans on the island. 'Maybe they're over there,' I suggested. 'They're swans, you idiot,' she snapped. She scrabbled off, and I thought of the ducks and drakes and gulls and pigeons and moorhens and swans, and who knows what else, that strutted their stuff around Richard's Pond. Did she think I was old Attenborough? By now, she was thirty yards away. I went after them and caught up with them at a bend. Gently ushering the little girl out of the way, I gave Grannie Greyhips a right good push, and in she went, into the pond –splash! 'Let me know if you see any sharks,' I shouted. And walked home. It really made my day, that incident. I mean, the pond is next door to a hospital, so she would have been all right."

"You better hope nobody saw you. You could be in real trouble this time. An old lady counts for more than an armchair, you know," warned Dave.

"Did you check behind you?" asked Calypso, and Franklin brushed this off with a "Yes, of course." But he knew he hadn't checked behind him.

He was not even half-drunk when he got home. Ruth had taken away a lot of items, and the flat seemed empty and hollow. When he dropped his keys, the sound echoed right along the corridor. He sat down and looked again at the phone number that would bridge the long gap between Franklin and Carmella. He propped it against a sugar bowl on the table and went to bed. But his mind would not sleep. He sat up with some pillows supporting him and let his mind go bobbing gently along, like that bottle in the Arena documentaries. Agnes was there, sitting on the couch beside him and telling him it was over. That serving years in prison as an accomplice to his terrible deeds was not her plan for her future. He refused to change, and he kept the same awful company, so she had started moves to divorce him. Carmella was with them, sitting across the room, watching him. Agnes and Carmella had just come back from a week's holiday in France. Agnes worshipped her mother-in-law and knew it would be hard to turn down any plea Carmella might make to postpone the divorce for a while. But Carmella did not make any plea. She sat in elegant silence, and Franklin's begging look across at his mother was in vain.

He had visited this memory often. *Why did Agnes leave?* he wondered, time after time. They had been married for only two years. He had used his cunning, his contacts and his natural fearlessness to provide enough income for them both to live well. She was a bit controlling and did not take to the semi-passive role that Franklin preferred for her. His father, Johnny, had at that point been long disappeared and never even knew Agnes. Agnes' parents were both dead, from a terrible error involving asbestosis. So two partners basically shared one parent. But that is an inaccurate picture of how things turned out. Agnes and Carmella started to live together. Franklin did not know, but his cousin, Giorgio, had discovered this unexpected development and had tried to tell Franklin in a serious, sensitive way. From the day in June 2011 that Franklin found this out, he had never spoken to his mother or his ex-wife. It was an additional stab to his heart that he had lost touch with Giorgio, who had once been the most important person in Franklin's world. Maybe he was someone else to add to the list of people he needed to phone.

Finally, Franklin fell asleep and slept right through until eight in the morning. By ten o'clock, he had completed some tidying up work online to get his accounts back in shape. At ten a.m. he called 07805 662214 and said, "Could I speak to Mrs Gaddarini, please?"

There was a short silence. He could hear quickened breathing.

"I'm sorry. You must have the wrong number."

"I don't think so. The lady I'm looking for could be now living under another name. I know her as Carmella Gaddarini. It's not a common name in Glasgow."

"Well, I can't help you. Who are you, anyway?"

"I am Franklin Gaddarini, her son. We haven't met for quite a long time."

"I'm sorry. I must go. Goodbye."

No, he could not be sure. He was not certain that the woman was his mother. More than a decade since they'd talked, her voice might well have changed. A lot of things would have changed, he guessed. What now? Be patient. There was no hurry. Then he remembered how untrue that was. Patrick, by now, was in a hurry. He had to get this job done very urgently.

For once, fate took a little pity on him. His phone rang. He answered. "Yes. Hello?" Far too quick and excited. It was the same woman.

"I am not the person you want, as I told you a little while ago. But I know about her. Before we proceed any further, you must answer two questions."

"Yes, yes – go ahead."

The first question is, what is your father's date of birth?"

Franklin was utterly taken aback. He regained composure, checked his memory for a minute and answered, "4 September 1948".

The second question again wrong-footed him. "What is the name of the Church your parents got married in?"

He would have to guess. His earliest memories of where they lived included the Church where he had been an altar boy. "The Good Shepherd Church," he said.

Now a different voice was heard; less smoky and more commanding, which came on with a low chuckle. "Well, well, well. Franklin. Franklin, my baby, has come back to his mother. There is a reason for that, absolutely no doubt, and it is probably a very unpleasant reason. Still, you were faultless on that little password test I just quickly made up. I'm pleasantly surprised you remembered the church – that was a hard one. So I tend for the moment to wait and see what you're about. You want us to meet? Or just to talk?

"I'd love to meet you. And thanks for not asking too many questions."

"Don't worry – that'll change. I'll give it some thought. For one thing, where are you?"

"I'm in Glasgow, but not in our old district."

"Ah, somewhere more elegant, I guess. I'll call you back quite soon. Goodbye."

Franklin's shirt was soaked with sweat. His eyes were watering, and his hands were shaking. His brain was in a spin. He had not realised what a volcanic move this might be. He stripped, took some deep breaths and then stood in the shower for some time.

Dried and dressed, he felt at the top of his crowded feelings, exhilaration. His mother! He had done it! His mother was alive and talking to him. She was not going to kill him. What next? Who knows? It was so thrilling.

He pulled out a big old trunk and opened it. He rummaged and found all manner of different things: a railway timetable to Girvan – exciting to think he and Carmella must have gone there together –some old clothes in a bundle, which turned out to be a Halloween costume, and a book called *The Hounds of Caprozzi*. Puzzled, he opened it. It was a boys' adventure war story set in Sardinia. It fell open at the first page, where a label was affixed. It said:

Saint Mungo's Academy 1989-90

Second Year Latin

First Prize: Giorgio Gaddarini

Franklin remembered how proud he had felt at that occasion. Giorgio, as has been noted earlier, was somewhat rough-and-tumble and very fond of getting into scrapes. To have won the prize for Latin in second year seemed an astonishing contradiction. But no,

Giorgio had had strong academic ability and maybe got a lot of enjoyment reading *Caesar's Gallic Wars*.

Franklin, transported back to happy days, came across lots of toys, games and puzzles and only two books. But there was nothing about or by his mother. And that railway timetable that had excited him at first had no names on it and could only be guessed at. But there was a pair of altar slippers that altar boys had to wear. He lifted them. They still looked brand-new. Not a speck.

His mother's face suddenly broke into his reveries, and he remembered, written on his heart with indelible ink, the evening in 1992 when Carmella had sat down with him and told him how life was about to change for both. She said her health was collapsing under the strain. Johnny, Franklin's dad, had disappeared a year before, and nothing was known. The police presented the usual sorrowful faces and earnest pledges to find him. Carmella told her son she was returning to Verona in Italy. Her mother had been begging her to do so in every phone call and letter. So she was going to go back for a while – perhaps six months or a year. She had spoken deeply with Marco Gaddarini, Johnny's brother, and his wife, Sophia. They, and Giorgio, of course, would look after Franklin until she returned, or maybe until he was old enough to come and join her. At present, she explained, it was impossible.

"You are at a good school, you are getting a fine education, and the teachers are clever and friendly. It would be a terrible risk and a sin to break up your education at this moment. Aunt Sophia has plenty of room. You will be able to take all your things over there."

"So this house – our house – is going to lie empty?"

"No, it's not. I have started a plan. It will be rented out on a short-term lease, maximum 6 months, so that when I am ready to come back, it will be easy to arrange things."

Giorgio was his hero then, so Franklin's pain did not last long. Two years passed, and Carmella, though she did keep in touch, showed no signs of recovering the health she said she needed to live in Glasgow.

The Gaddarinis became known around the school, and as Franklin started to grow and put on weight, he began to feel an equal with his cousin. They both had high profiles, and they were both popular. But Giorgio studied, and Franklin did not study. On the day of reckoning, Giorgio opened his envelope and found a certificate listing five Highers. Franklin half-pulled out the certificate to see only one pass – History.

That coincided with a very troublesome situation in Marco's house. Franklin's behaviour was usually acceptable for a lad of his age, in the circumstances he had, and Marco and Sophia made every allowance and excuse they could. But one day, Franklin came in early from school – no surprise – and feeling hungry, switched on the deep-fryer. And forgot about it. The ensuing fire destroyed half of the kitchen.

A few months later, Marco started giving Franklin driving lessons. On the second of these, Franklin reversed into a Honda Jazz and almost crumpled it.

Not long afterwards, he hinted that he would have to start looking around for work and might even have to move out and hoped they wouldn't mind.

They said, "What a pity, but go ahead; you might be lucky."

And when he went out, they had a little party.

Two nights later, around four a.m., Franklin tiptoed down with his haversack full. He crept into the back parlour where he knew Giorgio kept a little stash in a cubic biscuit tin. He took £100 and went on his way to meet Square-Eye and Bamba, who had acquired a wrecked car they said would get them to London.

At that point, Franklin came out of his reverie, stood up and strolled around the flat. What hit him right away was how clean and immaculate the whole apartment was. Furniture and bathroom basins gleamed, the air was wonderfully scented, and all the carvings and photos were tastefully placed: it was perfect. And it was all Ruth's doing – a little farewell gesture which, at least, he noticed. There was a little note placed on a small table. He read, 'Hope you know how to use this, or you're in more trouble.' Then he realised there were markings and inscribings on the little, round table. He played around a little and found there was a hinge that reversed the upper and lower sides. One was smooth and varnished, the other – which he had never seen before – seemed like it belonged in a séance parlour, or some such. He decided to leave it plain side up. He checked his watch – nearly twelve – surely time for a celebratory drink over at the local. Then he remembered his solemn vow: to reform himself and become a new man. Drinking at lunchtime would play no part in this new personality, he told himself as he strolled around the flat. Then he decided that such a moment – the reconciliation of a son with a mother – was surely an exception to any rule. He had to raise a glass to such an eventful day.

Some early lunchers were already at work with the fork and knife. The usual sprinkle of alkies were nursing their first lager or stout. Here, at least, life was predictable. Franklin knew where he was in the *Ewe and Lamb*. His lager was on the counter almost before he had ordered it. He went to a seat with a view of the door, so that when a pal entered to whom he wanted to tell the good news, he could wave him over.

After half an hour, this tactic had not proved successful, and he was still sitting on his own at one o'clock, an hour after he had come in. Onto his third pint, the day looked like it might crumble soon and mark his recent new start as a charade. The beer looked flatter now, and he began to muse a bit more deeply about the conversation. Who was the other woman? Were they equals, or who was in control? He would have recognised Agnes's voice right away. Maybe the number let you in to a cult or cultish group of women who lived together. Highly possible these days. Women riding around in posses, always on the lookout to round up men who infringed the new rules. They played games with men like passwords and riddles to disclose their identities. Franklin had usually found any urge to be paranoid was too tiring and called for too much brain activity. The people he knew who were most paranoid were also the most disappointed of people. It was just not worth the work. So he gave no further attention to who was at the end of the line.

Then in come Lou and Louie, the greatest music-hall act in those parts. Louie told everyone he had been at school with Franklin. He usually expressed it so that you didn't know if it was a boast or a confession. Franklin had no such memory, but he just agreed. With Lou and Louie, there was no chance of introversion or depth of discussion. They brought fun. Fun was their mission in life. So, glad of some company, Franklin closed the cupboard of important revelations and let himself sink into an afternoon of spicy food and spicy jokes. It was a long session during which he did make broken attempts to share his joy his reunion with his mother, but by then the timing was wrong, and the delivery was incoherent.

Chapter 21

The next morning, he was drinking coffee and feeling less hungover than he deserved. He thought it was his phone that rang, but it was the security door buzzer. He pressed the button.

"Good morning, sir," he heard. "Your car's here."

He recognised the mellow voice of Tamburlaine and instinctively said, "Give me five minutes."

They drove slowly over to *The Resting Place*. Tam even tried a joke, something about a man who built a pyramid but then couldn't remember the way in. Franklin paid little attention, trying to anticipate the grilling he was about to suffer.

Tam escorted him as far as the side corridor and pointed to the room at the bottom. It was the one with many divans. Patrick and Larry were close to the door and waved him in.

"Well, well, had a little holiday, eh? Did it do you good?"

"Well, a change of scene is always a good idea."

"Is that so? I wouldn't know. Larry, did you ever have the travel bug?"

Larry laughed and said he'd spent his life fighting bugs of all kinds.

"Franklin, let's not waste time. Your behaviour is worrying me. I sense a weakening of commitment on your part. The rather unusual work you are asked to do has its compensations, mainly in generous fees. Are you getting tired of supplying girls whose sensuality is balanced by their purity? Maybe you're not strong enough to deal with that. I placed you in a very pleasant job. And yes, the position did make some demands; required you to be charming and persuasive but never weak. Until recently, I felt justified in my appointing you. I am now doubtful. So I am proposing to move you to a quite different branch of the organisation. But before we get into that, perhaps we could bring some closure to this matter of your mother's address. If you have news, I'll hear it now."

"I have made progress. I have found her mobile phone number. But not yet her address. That will follow shortly, believe me. She is to call me soon, and that will be when we'll find out the address."

There was a pause as all three sat gathered in his own thoughts.

Patrick asked, "Are you fond of her? I suppose I should say, were you fond of her?"

"When I was young – at school – I was a bit afraid of her. She was so – just so different from us. It was like living with a different kind of being. Then, when my dad went, left, my mother withdrew even more into herself and locked me out. When she decided to go to Italy, to tell the truth, I was almost relieved. I thought me and Giorgio would have the time of our lives. And we did. But one result of that was that I sort of went to seed. I turned wild, and I took up with psychotic friends – the crazier, the better. I tried London and other places. But any time I felt I might stop and rest there, something inside me drove me on. No doubt these years would have been different if I had had a mother in my life."

Larry asked Franklin if he recognised what the something inside him was that drove him on.

"No. I just know it's been there for a long time. Maybe something like that Mr Hyde I read about. Certainly, it has his energies; energies that I myself do not have. I am a very slothful person."

"Yes," agreed Larry, "but maybe things can grow out of sloth."

Patrick seemed to feel they were getting off the main point and turned the discussion to another matter.

"You don't say much about missing your dad, though. As you say, he disappeared quite suddenly, did he not? That must have been a terrible shock for a young lad so fond of his father. At that time, or just in the year or two before it, I knew them both. Used to meet at Sunday Mass – you remember? Naturally, to you, I was just some other boring guy, so you paid no attention. Would you be surprised to know that your dad once worked for me? No, no – not the kind of work I ask you to do. Your dad would not have been suited to that. The work he did for me required nerve and strength and fearlessness. I regarded him as a stone in the stream. And then, just to vanish and not leave a trace or a hint of his going. It was troubling. It is still troubling."

Franklin did not see that this was a subtle form of interrogation. He began to relax and believed that the old guy had a soft spot for him and was only there to help.

"To the outsider, he was just another ordinary bloke. But as a dad, he was much better than ordinary. He made just enough for us to live on – we weren't poor or hungry. And now and again he would bring in a little surprise gift for me or mum, or usually both. I called them bonuses. I was happy then."

"The great mystery is why or how he vanished. Did you ever fear the worst – that he had been killed?"

"No, no, I didn't. It was too hard to think of anyone having a reason to kill him. Of course, somebody might have killed him accidentally and not wanted to tell anybody. A work accident, maybe."

"Were your parents getting on well at that time?"

"Yes, as far as I could tell. They had different views about lots of things and could snipe at one another, but never serious, that I heard."

Patrick turned in a stagey manner to Larry. "Larry, would you be a pal and find Tam and ask him to go down to the shop for a copy of *The Times*? That rascal has failed to deliver it again."

Larry seemed to leave without opening the door.

"I sometimes think Larry is our bat out of Hell. Now. Would you mind me asking you a more personal question? The answer might help us both with various difficulties we have."

"Sure. Go ahead."

"Well, I got to know your dad quite well, because I took the bus he drove, nearly every day. We became friends. Your mother was different. She did not see me with Johnny's openness. She was almost hostile; certainly suspicious."

"Of what? Of your intentions, as they say. She was suspicious that you could take her away from my dad. Now, that is crazy. Crazy. Sorry, I shouldn't say that. But to me it's so ridiculous."

This forceful reply surprised Patrick. He felt a strong resentment at the implication that he was in a lower league than an Italian bus driver and his wife.

"Well, being crazy is one way of staying out of Hell, so I hear. Anyway, as to the question I was going to ask: do you think maybe your dad could not cope with the pressure on him? And did much of that pressure come from your mother? When you think back – and I know it's a long, long time to recall – sometimes, although everything seems to be well, underneath that there is a deep human tension. And it can stretch only until it breaks – you know the expression about the straw that broke the camel's back. Could Carmella perhaps have stayed away from you all this time because of the guilt she feels about your father? And how she played a part in driving him away?"

"Well, that's a few questions. I'm wondering if I am seeing some plan at work here. You want to find her. You've asked me to help you. And so far, I haven't done enough. So you're trying to get into my brain and give me reasons why I need to find her and get back in touch with her."

"Well, treating me as a psychiatrist is flattering, but you're on the wrong path. Many secrets from the past are best left alone, but sometimes it's tempting to find out about mysterious things. We have some here."

"If I may ask you a question, what was the work that my dad did for you? You've never quite been clear about that."

"It was the way he wanted it. The chance of some extra income, to make life prettier for you and your mother, was hard to resist. But he was always scared of anything against the law or in bad taste. He respected the country's rules, he expected everyone to comply with them, and that had to include himself – he could not be hypocritical. He agreed to do a few manual jobs for me but insisted that we called the work 'fishing' if anybody asked. Mostly the work was at night, and I admit it had its unpleasant side, but I explained how a lot of successful fishing could be done at night. He was still 'fishing' right up to the time he disappeared."

"I remember I tried to follow him one night when he went out. I had heard that word fishing being used by him and my mother, and it puzzled me because there was very little water along that stretch of London Road."

"You followed him? Did he know you followed him?"

"No. He would have been angry. Anyway, I got tired, as well as scared. I realised I didn't want to know where the fish were. I turned and went back home. I never heard him come in."

"Yes, well, I suppose a lot would get lost in translation. That was wise. Ah, so many questions. So many unanswered questions. Listen, Franklin, you're probably a bit wary of me. Don't be. You got a sympathetic hearing when you attended the Committee meeting – or the Torch Committee, as we like to call it – gives it a little style. They are strict about judgements, and there is nothing I can do about a judgement made. I can help a bit, but I can't save you. Right. You have two recruits to find, for the middle and end of this month. Let's see you at your best in that project. Then if that goes well, I propose to offer you a sort of promotion. Different kind of work. More like your dad's in that it might involve you getting your hands dirty. Not everyone can do the job you're doing now. In fact, you look made for it. But Larry, for example, could never really do your job. But it's not the only job you could do, and I've been wondering whether a change would do you good. Think about that. But it's still first things first."

"I'll just add, that for reasons unknown, my dad left suddenly and went back to his hometown in Italy. He's still in Italy. Why he had never got in touch with me remains a mystery. One day it will be revealed."

"Wouldn't that be wonderful, Franklin. I pray hard and often that it proves to be the truth."

Silence swirled around for a few seconds.

"You're a Catholic, Franklin. You remember that phrase in the Creed we say at Mass – 'the resurrection of the body'. I don't think that phrase gets the attention it deserves. Most Catholics don't know what to make of it. I mean, we're all going to be risen in Christ –at least, some of us. No problem there. But a bodily resurrection? You can see right away the kinds of problems that might bring. I can see over nearly the whole graveyard from one of my upper windows, and how often I have stood there and tried to picture the tombstones starting to shake and topple, the turf bursting up and peeling back and what rough beasts come forth on the day of Resurrection."

"Maybe it's you that needs a holiday, Patrick, not me. Mind you, I don't recommend holidays. They're just not what they're cracked up to be. By the way, I still haven't been told why you need the address. Wouldn't the phone number be enough?"

"People can lie on the phone and usually do. You must have noticed that. But if you see where they live, you can find out a lot. Then the next stage is getting inside the address—"

"When you say stage, it makes all this sound like a careful plan."

"Don't you go getting concerned about plans. Plans are not your thing. I do need Carmella's address. Keep that in front of your mind when you get distracted. This time, I'm not going to put any target date on the task. You must get it done. Tam's in the corridor – he'll see you out. Be careful with the tombs."

He sat at his computer and started checking out some possibilities. There were two which looked suitable: a forty-year-old named Greta who looked very clever, but maybe a little too slim; and a red-haired woman named Celia, who said she loved playing the violin to small groups or gatherings – that could be developed. His diary check showed him he had seven and ten days, respectively, to hook in these recruits. The fishing image made him think for a moment of his dad and his fishing escapades. *Ain't life strange*, he thought.

Within a short time, he was reeling in Celia, enthusing about violin music and assuring her the club was the ideal platform for her to perform in. Of course, it would have to be in addition to the other matters required of her in the arrangement. She seemed most enthusiastic. He asked her to put 8th May in her diary.

He decided that left him space to leave Greta for a few days. That was Franklin – he never completed anything but always left something trailing.

He took two pills and went to bed and slept for more than twenty-four hours. He woke up and saw it was midday Saturday. His first thought was that there was an important football match being played that night, and he would get over to the pub and watch it in peace with a few buddies. He was not an ambitious person.

Chapter 22

He was looking at the large TV screen, but he was watching a woman at the bar. He had caught only the most flashing of glimpses when she had passed by seconds before. Now he watched. He recognised the contours, the height, the self-assured posture and the habit of standing with one ankle wrapped around the other. His suspicions were correct. He saw her heading straight at him with a glass in her hand, shades on her eyes and some white teeth showing – Agnes.

"Hello, Franklin. Now who do you think will win? The game, I mean."

She gave a smile. "Sorry, boys, could I take Frankie away from you for a few minutes? We have a sort of tribal feud to deal with, not to mention a world war to finish." Another smile, and the barflies gaped in wonder and astonishment.

They went across to an empty table, and Franklin decided to get straight to business. He knew that letting her take the lead by asking questions would be calamitous, as it had been so many times, twelve years ago. So he said, "I know someone who wants to meet someone you know. Is this a meeting you have come here to arrange?"

"Well, very commanding and very direct, eh? Darling Franklin, don't have me say this too many times – you weren't born to make speeches. But to your interesting opening gambit, I will respond with this – a friend of mine wants to know the address of someone you work for."

Franklin understood. Mr Patrick was at the centre of everything, it seemed. He did not know why they wanted Patrick's address, and he realised he did not know why Patrick wanted Carmella's address, although he could make a guess. So in this divided state of mind, he pulled back from the attack; withdrew his opening pawn, as it were.

"Agnes, let's leave all this for a minute, can we?

"Sure we can. Drink up. But listen; that's amazing – your scar is gone. Amazing! So you never went for vanity surgery!"

"I'm kinda low on vanity, but I do have other sins. And – I've got other scars if you want to see them."

"Let me get you another beer."

"No, no, I'll do that. Is that vodka? He called a waiter and ordered drinks.

"Yes, it is, Franklin. I got tired of gin when they started putting seaweed or pink 'Tizer in it. Good vodka is a lot straighter. Remember what it did to President Yeltsin?"

Franklin's eyes were blank, and his mouth was still.

"Sorry, darling; I forgot you don't keep up with current affairs."

For once he was able to score a point. "Agnes, you look wonderful. Whatever it is you're having for breakfast, pass the secret on."

He was right, and her smile was a knockout. On looks, a shot of them sitting there, close and still friendly, would have made the cover of any glamour magazine.

"And is it true, as I heard a while ago, that you and Carmella are living together?"

"We are living together. That cannot be denied. But how it is interpreted is a more complex thing. So before you start lathering up with saucy images of intertwined lesbians writhing in ecstasy; one of them your mother, and the other your ex-wife – I can see you now. Oh, boy, wish I'd been there when you first heard the news. Life is 90% mundane drudgery – haven't you learned that yet, Frankie boy? Carmella is quite well after a bout of ill health a year ago. In fact, she's flourishing. And I am, as you see. You've kept your condition quite well, too; the benefit of those three years you spent with me among the volcanoes of married bliss.

Franklin moved a little closer, but Agnes placed a hand firmly on his thigh.

"No, no, Franklin. The answer is no. Let us get that clear. Any more improper advances, and I'll tell your mother. It does sound so funny, you must admit."

"That's OK, I wasn't... I'm just a bit bowled over, you appearing out of the blue and, if I remember, into a pub you once said you'd love to set on fire."

She chuckled. "I forgot about that. I'll have to add it back on the list. And I could add, you're on that list. I still think getting set on fire is too good for you, except for that underworld fire that lasts forever. Meantime, we need your help. And I understand that you need ours. So this is going to be tricky for you, Frankie boy."

Franklin thought back to their time together, and how what she loathed most about him was his slothfulness and passivity; how he spent days getting ready to do things that never happened; how he would sit in a lively group conversation with friends and say nothing till the very end, when he would contribute some gnomic remark that was supposed to be cool and definitive. She could stand him a little more when he was positive and in control of an event or a situation. His good looks were a given bonus, but he did not think that asset would work very strongly now. He decided to go for cynical and unconcerned.

Agnes took off her coat.

"You work for a person you know as Patrick. We found out because a person whom we know now also works for Patrick and wants out. He, too, is a C member – does that mean something to you? Yes? Anyway, this Patrick did very serious wrong to your mother and your late father. He drove a wedge between your mother and father. He connived in the death of Johnny Gaddarini. I didn't know Johnny, of course – he had been fourteen years disappeared when we got married. I tried to get you to talk about him, but you wouldn't, or maybe you just couldn't. When Carmella did get to know some of the truth about Patrick, she had no idea where you were, so when you phoned, she could hardly believe how fortune had thrown her this card; you coming back into her life – the person she needs to get to Patrick."

"Don't you think all this Patrick stuff is weird? I mean, what's his second name? Who is he?"

"His name is Patrick DiNardo."

"DiNardo…Gaddarini. God, they seem to belong together somehow. It's creepy."

Franklin had regretted their divorcing. But the warning signs were there, and he did nothing to change the causes of that parting. He felt emotionally confused, now, in her company, finding himself recalling some good times they had. This was a terrible decision, a terrible choice. His brain was objecting, not being practised in this kind of work.

Agnes had much stronger brain control even when, like now, for a moment she saw the languid beauty in Franklin, marvellously offset by the shadow of the little scar on his jaw. For an instant, the old passion roared through her. But it was not hard to get it back under lock and key.

They took a break from the main course and dipped into a few others. Agnes noticed his company hadn't changed – a predictable, lowlife gang of misfits with adopted names like Feather or Bintang or Buster. He observed that the new, black eyeshadow really suited her. She told him his pointed shoes were hellish and advised a particular shop where he could get some good ones. But they were circling back to the main matter of the addresses.

Franklin asked, "Why do you want his address, anyway? You planning to launch an attack?"

"The same reason you want Carmella's address. Is old DiNardo going to come and surround our house?"

"Ok, come on, Agnes, we could go round and round all night. Let's each write down the address, and we pass it over to one another at the same moment."

"I can go with that." She opened her handbag and took out a little notepad. She tore off two pages and gave one to Franklin. On the other, she wrote her address. Then she passed the pen to Franklin, who wrote down Patrick's address. The pen was returned. Then, at the same moment, they slid their sheets across the table, and each looked at the address before them.

"37 Prospect Terrace, Glasgow, G42 4TP. Isn't that down near the river Clyde?

"No. It's nowhere near the Clyde; it's well south of the river. And yours says *The Resting Place*, 1 Nostrum Crescent, Glasgow G61 6LL. Where the hell is that?"

"It's north, right beside The Levels private cemetery. You'll have to find it on Google. You're not getting any more."

"Ok. Don't get touchy. Beside a private cemetery. That's very interesting. I know what Carmella will say. She'll say that somewhere in that private cemetery, her lovely Giovanni is hidden. And what about you – where are you staying? Don't tell me you're still in the old place!"

"Nah, I moved about six years ago. I have a second-floor, three-bedroom, fully equipped studio flat in the desirable area of Kelvin, precisely at number 7 Lemon Lane, G12 0SM."

"Nice. Lemon Lane. Never heard of it. I'll write that down, too. Maybe I could come up and visit you sometime if all this goes well?

"You mean that?"

She passed him a beautiful smile.

"Now, Carmella suggested if we reach any agreement here, we could arrange a short meeting in some bar in Merchant City. You OK with that? You have any preference there?"

"Well, there's the *Metropolitan* and *O'Hanlon's,* but that's a bit rough. Maybe *Panellis* would be good."

"OK. One of us will phone you tomorrow with a day and time. Are we controlling too much of this, Franklin?"

"Maybe you are. I'm just thinking – very shortly, I'll be giving Mr Patrick your address, as he requested, and I'll see his reaction. Then I should phone you and see what the next step is."

"The next step in what? This isn't a stage opera. You give him the address, and you better get outta there. Either that, or dive for cover inside."

"No, no, you don't know him. He'll be calm, he'll be very happy, and he'll propose some pleasant celebration. I'm sure he'll invite you both, and who knows what new beginnings we can look forward to."

"Jesus, Franklin, you really should have gone to school."

They stood up, and she gave him a warm hug and stood watching as he looked at his place on the upholstered bench, then looked over at his buddies, then looked back through half-closed eyes at Agnes.

But he got another drink, went over, sat down and asked, "What's the score, Buster?"

"Ah, think it's 1-0."

At that moment, from behind Agnes appeared the figure of Brother Alphonsus, one of several local Franciscan medicant monks, who regularly raided the local pubs fearlessly for donations. There was always a little banter, which the monk took in his stride and gave as much as he got. As he got closer, Franklin felt a deep gripping below his lungs, as if his liver had been shifted round by about ten degrees.

As Alphonsus arrived, Franklin said, "*Sacerdotis te cito venisti mihi.*"

The monk replied in a calm voice, "*Tempus enim prope est tuum in finem.*"

More than six people were within the hearing of this.

Buster exclaimed, "Hell and damnation, Frankie; what the bloody Hell is that about? We're tryin' tae watch a game here."

Agnes turned back with astonishment on her face. She was taken aback, and she sat down on a seat close to, but out of sight of Franklin's party. She saw Alphonsus leave the bar, his bag jingling but, his face inscrutable within his hood.

Franklin resumed watching the football. Roberto gave his arm a friendly squeeze. The game finished 2-2, and the pundits agreed it was a good, exciting game. But it did not leave Franklin in anything like a state of excitement. A few people drifted off after the game and allowed Franklin to slither over towards the barber. Only a four-inch partition separated him from Agnes, who was sitting calmly with her eyes closed, waiting and picking up every word of the following conversation.

"Buster, I need to talk to somebody. Have you got a few minutes?"

Buster nodded warily.

"Remember a while ago we were talking, and you were telling me about your mother and how you were scared of what she might do in her will?"

"Aye, ah remember. It wis only last week."

"Has she made a will?"

"Naw, ah doubt it. It's no' her style."

"So by law, if she died, everything comes to you, the eldest son."

"Aye, but when's she gonny die?"

Franklin lowered his voice. "Maybe you could affect that. Have you ever thought of killing her? Your mother?

"No, I bloody well have not. What put that into your head? Franklin, you're a psycho, you know that. You got no mother that anybody knows about, and you go around giving advice to your mates about how to kill their mother? Jesus!"

"Actually, I have got a mother, and she's been in touch with me."

"So you gonny kill her? What, for reappearing out of the mists of time? I do remember you had some pretty bad things to say about her."

"Buster, I don't know why I still talk to you. You have no world view of anything."

"Eh?"

Chapter 23

Franklin, the next morning, was eating some porridge with prunes. He put down the spoon and concentrated. He knew he was caught between two forces. Carmella would phone that day. But maybe later. Meantime, he could make contact with Mr Patrick, so that when he went to the meeting with Carmella, he would have a good idea where he stood with the opposing force. On the other hand, what Carmella chose to reveal to him might alter his view of Mr Patrick entirely, even to the extent that he decides to cut all ties with Patrick and throw his fate into the arms of his mother, so to speak. Neither the porridge, nor the prunes had offered sound advice. He made coffee, opened his balcony onto a lovely Spring morning and stood and waited.

The phone rang, and he answered.

"Hello, Franklin. This is Carmella. Hope you're well this morning. What do you say to dinner tomorrow night? I suggest *Bernardo's* in Queen Street. D'you know it?"

"I do, yes."

"What about 7.15 then, Monday 6th? Lovely. I'm excited. Oh, in case I forget – will you be coming alone?"

"Of course, Mother. Don't we have personal things to discuss?"

"Yes, but in case there's someone you're close to, like Agnes and me, it would be quite all right to bring her. Or him."

"Well, I doubt it. But thanks for the suggestion. With just the three of us, there's less chance of a brawl breaking out. See you tomorrow night. Bye."

"Ooh, wouldn't that be fun!"

She was still laughing that low laugh when she hung up. That was it.

He had a few drinks at the *Ewe and Lamb*, both in the afternoon and again around nine p.m., but his mind was elsewhere.

It took quite a few seconds for the eyes to adjust to *Bernardo's* idea of lighting. It was dark, in a shadowy way, with strange Sicilian puppets hanging in alcoves and from the ceiling, their expressions covering the whole range, the most terrifying being a broken-toothed hag who hung just above and behind Carmella, where she was sitting next to Agnes. They both rose when the waiter brought Franklin over to them, and Carmela and her son embraced. It was emotional. Each of them was shaking. Agnes advised that they all sit down, and that proved most welcome.

"Well, son, it's been a lotta years; a lotta tears, too. But let me look at you. Franklin, you're as beautiful as ever. More so! *Dio mio*, how did I produce a god like you? Oh, and look – just like a god – you've got a scar. Here, at your jawline. It's quite sexy."

Agnes eyes were wide. She came over and looked closely and saw that the scar was indeed where it had always been since Franklin received it in a fight in London in his younger days.

"It's come back, Franklin. How strange!" she said quietly. "Maybe I was wrong."

"Maybe. But scar or not, I'm no god, and you probably know that already, if I remember you. On the other hand, look at you – a divine elegance glows in the darkness of this place. I think somebody else wrote that. But you are breathtaking. No wonder Agnes made a bid you couldn't refuse."

That was a good icebreaker, and they all laughed merrily. Nobody wanted a starter course, so they were still talking ultra-safely about events and people they'd known, when the main course plates were collected. They all took dessert, and at that point began to focus on business.

Carmella spoke first. "You know, from your dad, how many Italians came to Glasgow and set up trade in the ice-cream shop or the fish and chip shop. DiNardo – let's forget Patrick – was from such a family. His father, Paolo, did well in the Tally Shop but was obsessed with getting his son – Patrick – to do better – to rise in the city and be a man of influence. Maybe he got his wish, although he died a couple of years ago. Anyway, DiNardo stopped at nothing – the classic case of a man willing to climb over the bodies of his peers to get past them to the top. He got to know your father, and through him, he saw me, and he decided he must have me. At first, he was just a pest. But then he became a curse. He was subtle and cool. He knew Giovanni was on a low wage, so he tempted him, with money, to take part in some very vile and evil work. Before I tell you about it, let me ask you; do you like DiNardo?"

"Like? No. His style and his swagger are obvious, but he's not likeable. Bit like Dad. Maybe. I work for him to earn money. He pays me well. So I treat him as an employer. But I've always found him creepy. I came home from school once and saw you and him sitting in the living room with wine and an art book on the table. I felt a bit nauseous then – at the two of you – and for ages I worried about it. DiNardo has been talking to me about Dad and trying to find out how much I know about the night shift work he did back then."

"Did he tell you what this night shift work really was? I'm sure you must have known it wasn't anything to do with fishing."

"I always believed anything Dad told me. It seemed odd, but I did believe him. But not strongly enough to tell anybody."

"Giovanni always had very strong religious beliefs. He didn't force them on anyone. But he was proud to be a Catholic. Are you a Catholic, Franklin?"

"A very poor example of one, but yes; I'm on the side of the angels."

Agnes expressed some amused surprise at this claim. "Then you've really changed. I used to think of you often as a demon, or at least a friend of demons."

"I blame myself a lot for that. I've often worried that I did not raise you properly enough in our religion. Maybe that's why you drift so much from the faith."

"I drift from everything, Mother. Is all this religious discussion necessary?"

There was a long pause of silence.

"Have you come across the term 'body-snatchers'?

"Dad was a body-snatcher?"

"Not exactly, Franklin. But that was the business DiNardo was in. Gangsters in this city needed a quick and reliable place to get rid of bodies where they would not be found. It was an Italian who suggested to them the best place was in a cemetery; choose a grave where the occupant was surely skeletal, dig up the grave, take out the skeleton, and put in the victim. The Italians who were involved got well rewarded in money and in protection. A lot of graves in Glasgow graveyards contain people whose names are not on the headstones. I believe the cemetery used most in this horrible business was a private graveyard.

"So Dad was one of the gravediggers. And, presumably, somebody else took care of the corpse amid the bones."

"Of course. The bones went into very sterile and sealed metal boxes. Once the body was in place, Giovanni and his partner had to replace the coffin and cover it with soil and then with the turf, or whatever lay on the top of the ground. I have no idea what they did with the skeletons."

There was a gloomy silence for a while, then Franklin said, "I remember, once, the garden shed was left unlocked, and I was curious to see what was inside. It was shadowy, but I saw a strange-looking container; some sort of oddly shaped metal thing."

"Yes, you're right. His tools were in that box – all short-handled, because of the limited space for digging. There was one time when Giovanni made a mess of the job. He started filling in the grave, and only then realised the dead man – a very small man in this case – was still lying on the grass beside the grave. He panicked. His partner saw what had happened, rolled the body into the half-filled grave, and they managed to cover the body with less than two feet of soil. Fortunately, there was a horizontal slab of stone to be slid over it. The episode really upset him. I nearly had a heart attack when he vividly described the whole event to me. Then he broke down under the strain of it all, burst into tears, then rage and anger. Said he was going to kill the beast, DiNardo. He raved all night like a madman. In the morning he looked calm – up, as usual, for his shift, drinking his tea quietly and eating toast. I hugged him and asked was he all right. 'I am fine, Carmella', he said, and left for work. I never saw him again."

"Maybe it's up to me to revenge my father's death. Are you sure he is dead?"

"How can I be? He vanished completely. You remember your father. Just think back for one moment. Is it possible that he could be alive and not contacted you, or me? It's impossible. I know DiNardo was involved. He was the hand behind the murder of your father. Now, once again, he's after me. Maybe he wants to kill me too. For refusing him all this time. And you – you're just a pawn in his game. He'll easily get rid of you. I hear he lives right beside a graveyard. How convenient."

Franklin realised, more than his mother, how true this was, with his mansion overhanging The Levels cemetery. It occurred to him that, in that cemetery, his beloved father might be buried, replacing some poor skeleton who had been resting there for many decades. It was all beginning to overwhelm Franklin.

He took a moment to study his mother. Her beauty was even richer now in middle age, and her eyes retained all the old power of command. She was surely still more than a match for Patrick. She could handle him. But she was telling him how her life had been damaged by this man Patrick, and she was seeking revenge for her suffering. She was asking him to end her suffering.

"Franklin, we've been apart so many years. Maybe we could still restore our life a little."

"It's a nice idea, I agree. But I don't see how, with you two..."

Agnes was ready. "Oh, Franklin. Yes, you and I could still have a fling. I fling either way."

"Agnes, you're wicked!" said Carmella.

"Is that so bad?" asked Agnes, and they both laughed. Franklin wondered at their laughter at this point. A terrible thought flew through his brain, but it was gone before he could examine it.

"And I think I'm speaking for Carmella there, too. We could have a great time. Frankie, admit it, you're still drifting; you're achieving nothing. Here's a great offer. A marvellous deal."

Then it was back to Carmella. "Franklin, until you turned up from nowhere, I always had this terrible shadow hanging over me. DiNardo had stalked me for years, just for his fun, and I saw no hope. I've moved house time after time, and he always finds me. He killed my beloved Giovanni, and from what I gather, he is now destroying my son with his depraved projects."

"I'm going to see him. What happens when I meet him, I don't know. I'll have to improvise. Maybe I'll just give him your address and leave."

"Franklin." She took his hands in hers and caressed them. "You'll come up with something better than that.

It's now or never, for this business to end. Fate has brought us together to do this and will reward us if we show courage and gratefully accept the gift that fate is bestowing upon us."

There was a blast wave of pressure coming at Franklin from the women. He needed just a little time.

"I'll phone DiNardo, go and see him, and then I'll phone you. With good news, I hope."

Agnes had tears in her eyes. "We're in your hands, Franklin."

But he did not phone right away. He went down to the pond and sat on a bench, aware of a few people going along. He imagined a 'Wanted' poster pinned to a tree, with his face and a notice saying, 'This man pushed an old lady into the pond'. He tried to chuckle at the image but found the joke too sour. He took a deep breath. What on earth to do? Who could he trust?

Was there anyone who might at last provide some meaning and insight into Franklin's plight?

"Hello, Tommy. Is that you? I'm so glad I got you."

"Franklin, hello there. We're just off on a retreat for a week, so—"

"No, no, Tommy, it's all right. I'm not planning another visit just now. I have a difficult question to deal with. I thought the person who might help me is your brother, Robert. I wanted to speak to him. Could you let me have his phone number?"

"Of course I could," answered the relieved Tommy. "Sure I have it off by heart."

He read it out to Franklin, who copied it into his phone.

"Thanks a million, Tommy. A great help. Sorry about the rush here. I'll be in touch."

"Trubba not, Frankie. I'm glad. I mean, I'm sorry you can't get away right at the minute. Bye. I'll pray for you at Loch Neigh. And whatever it is, I'm sure Robert will be of help to you."

Franklin punched in Robert's number, but it went straight to his voicemail. He tried a few times without success. The third time, he asked Robert if he would call Franklin back as soon as he could and left it at that.

Franklin did not waste any further time. He called Patrick, said he finally had information for him and was calling to arrange a date to visit. Patrick seemed excited.

"No need for appointments this time. There's nobody here now. Can you come over now?"

He parked outside the drive and walked for a little while among the tombs. He tried to come up with a story that might frighten Patrick; that Carmella had big information on him; that she was going to expose the Club for the evil deeds behind its pious facade; that she had got the police to reopen the case of her missing husband; but that she'd be willing to meet him to come to some arrangement. He would decide which of these to use, depending on how the meeting went. Thus, heavily armed, he rang the doorbell of his nemesis.

"That you, Franklin? Come in. Second left at top of staircase."

Franklin looked up and saw Patrick standing at the top of the staircase. Here was the fiend they had been discussing – a white-haired, monkish figure who went to Mass every morning, who had paid Franklin a good salary for three years and who simply wanted to renew an old acquaintance. Perhaps Franklin would have stayed with this image if Patrick had not jolted him out of it by his opening remarks. He beckoned Franklin upwards.

"Franklin, it's decision time. You have a final choice. Either you have an interesting life working in security for me, or you live forever pestered by a woman who has lost her mind."

Already he had taken Franklin by the elbow and was ushering him through the door.

"You don't want the address?"

"It's OK. I already know it. I had you followed. Then I had them followed. You have a lot to learn."

"I'm not the only one," Franklin said on the turn, and struck out with his left arm. The power of it seemed almost supernatural to Franklin. The arm hit Patrick full in the face and sent him hurtling down the stairs, limbs whirling, to a full stop, where the back of Patrick's head collided with an ivory umbrella stand.

Franklin sat down on the top stair. He was not even out of breath, yet his blow had sent Patrick spinning through the air to a ghastly thud on the hallway floor.

He let some time pass, until it began to dawn on him that DiNardo might be dead. He would have to check. He was very fearful and still did not move. No hurry – the place was empty, Patrick had said. And yet, something would have to be done. It had been an accident. But how would it be seen? By others? By the police and the court? He felt chilled and more and more alone. He would have to go down there and look.

He rose and tiptoed down the stairs. He looked. Patrick was dead. His eyes were open and looking up the stairs. Franklin made a burst for the small bathroom on the right, was sick and almost wet himself. The water splashing on his face helped calm him, and he returned to the hall and approached the body more closely. Yes, he was dead. No question.

He paced around, and then realised he would feel less isolated if he phoned his mother. And suddenly, he could not wait to call Carmella and lift the ancient burden from her life. He did so, and he heard her weep with joy and gratitude over the phone. Three times she asked him was it true, was he dead, how did he know for sure? Then Agnes took over the phone and asked the same questions.

"I should call the police, Agnes. It was an accident. A complete accident."

"Don't be an idiot, Franklin. How will it look? You and Carmella have grudges against the old guy. You leave here and go over there; next thing he's dead. They'll never believe you. Look, make sure you leave nothing there – not a hair or a fingerprint. Get a rag, wipe everything, then leave and take the rag with you. Don't leave it there. And come back here. We can discuss the next move then. Don't waste any time – somebody is sure to turn up soon."

Franklin found a store cupboard and some cloths inside. He wiped any places he thought he might have touched and was so busy running the cloth over the end of the banister that he did not see who was standing beside the body.

"Well, well, well. Our leader has fallen, it seems," said Larry to a woman beside him, whom Franklin did not know. "And just after he had instructed me to find another resting place. And do you know, Jenny, he told me we might need two lairs. You see, that was the vision of the man."

He turned to Franklin.

"Franklin, at least do me the courtesy due from one villain to another. We're all guilty, Franklin, and we all must pay for our sins. You remember Brother Kurt? Yes. He's hoping to be promoted to assistant chief constable next month. Think how upset he will be at the passing of our old friend, Patrick. How could he let such a death go unpunished and still hope to be elevated within the great police force that we are proud of here in Glasgow?"

He turned to the woman beside him and ushered her towards Franklin. She spoke, but to Franklin her voice seemed of smoke rather than expelled air.

"You still look so good, Franklin. Nobody would guess, looking at you, what you've been through - what you've put yourself through. You remember me, don't you?"

"You're vaguely familiar, but no, I don't quite recognise you."

"Jenny. At your wedding – remember? I was Agnes's bridesmaid."

"Yes, but – how did you get here? You used to tease me; used to warn me about Agnes – I'm so confused. Jenny. Yes. But what are you doing here?"

"I'm here as a witness. Just as I was at your wedding. Now at another very significant moment, I am here again."

Looking over her shoulder, Franklin saw that the hall was starting to fill with other people, or at least, other shapes: dark and shadowy; slowly shifting along towards him; faces unseen; almost forming a single entity coming to embrace him.

He heard the voice of Larry intone, "His lair awaits, below, below."

And Franklin ran. He had a good start, and he knew the grounds well. Above all, he recalled the tree-lined walkway at the back. He headed that way. He caught his breath and slowed his pace within the arbour.

At that moment, his phone rang. He looked but did not recognise Robert's number. Then he heard one of them calling his name, and in a rushed moment, he burst out through the end of the walkway, onto the green slope of the steep lawn that ran down to the water, unimpeded. Franklin, too, was unimpeded as he hurtled down wildly and hit the black waters of the quarry lake, both arms outstretched, as if perhaps in a dive. Something was on his face that might have been a grin rather than a smile. From the disturbed waters, an unpleasant waft of sulphur swirled briefly across the air. Within seconds, there was neither sight of Franklin, nor sound. His body drifted down and down and into the caves below, where some old hemp cloth from an ancient piece of machinery wound itself gently around him, creating a kind of burial shroud.

That is where his body arrived at. As to his soul, that is a more difficult question.

CHAPTER 24

Agnes was suggesting that they try avocado with their smoked salmon and scrambled eggs, but Carmella was not really listening. When Agnes noticed this, she asked what was on her friend's mind.

"It is strange that you ask that, Agnes, is it not? It's only about an hour since my son delivered me from that little creep. And now where is Franklin gone? And you ask what's on my mind? Certainly not avocado, anyway."

"That's over two hours, Carmella. Franklin should have phoned us."

"He was never a very predictable boy. I never knew when he was going to turn up, or when he was going to disappear for – well, who could tell? Weeks, months… He never found someone to look after him like he needed – no insult intended to you, darling; you did your best with the beast in him. But we can only take so much. Agreed? Try calling him again."

"No luck. Phone's dead."

"I'm getting this feeling I got that day Giovanni left us. A dread in my stomach, that he was not coming back. I'm beginning to feel that again. Now."

"I'll tell you this, Carmella. I knew, when he left here, I would never see him again."

"Isn't it awful?"

Agnes's phone rang. She whispered to Carmella, "It's Jenny."

Her face was still as a slab as she took in Jenny's news. She put the phone down and said, "She said he'd run towards the water. Jenny had run after him, but he was too far ahead. He went straight under the surface and did not reappear."

"Water? What water? Franklin never went near water. Dear, dear. Is Jenny coming over? Did she say?"

"No, but she said she'd phone again if she got more information."

"OK. Listen. Leave the food just now. I'm not very hungry, are you? Put your coat on, and we'll take a walk over and put some flowers on Giovanni's grave. We'll have to tell him the news."

The events of this tale of Franklin Gaddarini occurred one Eastertide, in the springtime of the year. Perhaps resurrection is not for everyone.